D0378919

YELLOW

BY THE SAME AUTHOR

Sex Education

YELLOW

JANNI VISMAN

Viking

VIKING
Published by the Penguin Group
Penguin Group (USA) Inc., 375 Hudson Street, New York, New York 10014,
U.S.A. • Penguin Group (Canada), 10 Alcorn Avenue, Toronto, Ontario,
Canada M4V 3B2 (a division of Pearson Penguin Canada Inc.) • Penguin Books
Ltd, 80 Strand, London WC2R 0RL, England • Penguin Ireland, 25 St.
Stephen's Green, Dublin 2, Ireland (a division of Penguin Books Ltd) • Penguin
Books Australia Ltd, 250 Camberwell Road, Camberwell, Victoria 3124, Aus-
tralia (a division of Pearson Australia Group Pty Ltd) • Penguin Books India Pvt
Ltd, 11 Community Centre, Panchsheel Park, New Delhi – 110 017, India • Pen-
guin Books (NZ), Cnr Airborne and Rosedale Roads, Albany, Auckland 1310,
New Zealand (a division of Pearson New Zealand Ltd) • Penguin Books (South
Africa) (Pty) Ltd, 24 Sturdee Avenue, Rosebank, Johannesburg 2196, South Africa

Penguin Books Ltd, Registered Offices: 80 Strand, London WC2R 0RL, England

First American edition
Published in 2005 by Viking Penguin, a member of Penguin Group (USA) Inc.

10   9   8   7   6   5   4   3   2   1

Copyright © Janni Visman, 2004
All rights reserved

LIBRARY OF CONGRESS CATALOGING IN PUBLICATION DATA
Visman, Janni
  Yellow / Janni Visman.
    p. cm.
  ISBN 0-670-03402-9
  1. Paranoia—Fiction. I. Title
  PR6122.I86Y45 2005
  813'. 6—dc22 2004061183

This book is printed on acid-free paper. ∞

Printed in the United States of America
Designed by Carla Bolte • Set in Granjon with Akzidenz Grotesk

In my ideal life I am arranged alphabetically.
And I am never infected with nostalgia.

The rules I made when he moved in:

No stories from the past.
No unnecessary anecdotes.
No questions.

"Suits me fine," he said.

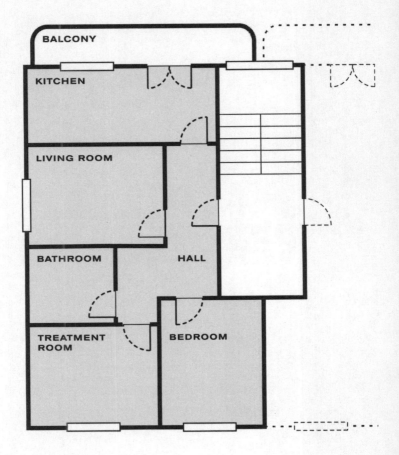

TUESDAY

The room is full of the smell of oranges. Ivan is already down to the pith, the continuous spiral of peel on the table in front of him. Up till a moment ago, we were neck and neck, but then my peel broke and I had to refind my purchase. Up till a moment ago, it was perfect symmetry. We take our time with the pith, let it get under our nails. I speed up a little to be in sync with him again. The oranges are fresh; the pith comes off in large sections. We both pile it to the right of the peel. The next part of the ritual, the part before we sink our thumbs into the center to split the fruit apart, is to push up our sleeves. First we put the orange down on the plate. Then we push the sleeve on the left arm up. Then the right arm. Gentle, domestic maneuvers.

We watch each other as we do this. Content in our predictability.

It glints in the morning sunlight and sends its reflection across the kitchen ceiling and across my face. A gold bracelet. In the time he's been living with me, he's never worn jewelry. Instinctively, I wrap my hand around his wrist across the table and draw it toward me.

"Show me," I say.

A gold ID bracelet. His name is engraved on it in italics: *Ivan.* There are a few scratches and indentations on the surface of the piece where the name is. The links are chunky on his skinny wrist. It makes his wrist look like a child's. He tries to pull away. Sheepish, angry and shy all at the same time. I am indignant.

"Let me see."

I yank his wrist closer and twist the bracelet around to find the catch. The gaps between the links trap the hair as I slide it around, and he winces.

"Sorry." I try to be more careful but am impatient.

"Don't be so rough," he says.

"Don't be such a baby!" I say.

The catch is fiddly. It seems too small and delicate for the size of the thing. I need to use my nails. The bits of pith do not make matters easier. It finally opens, and the bracelet falls into a heap between us on the table. Its sound is weak despite its size. A dull thud. Ivan draws back his hand and rubs his bare wrist.

"It's just a bracelet."

"I can see that."

As if he has suddenly changed his mind about letting me

inspect it, Ivan tries to snatch at it. I get there before him. I cup it close against my chest.

"Secrets?"

He leans back into his chair, rolls his eyes into the back of his head and folds his arms. I move my hand away from my chest slightly but keep it close. The bracelet feels light. I see a hallmark. It indicates twenty-four karat, but the bracelet feels more like nine. In fact, it feels like it could be gold-plated. Then I see the inscription on the back of the panel. It's in the same italics as his name, but smaller. Ivan has taken to rolling the orange around his plate, not sure of whether to start eating it or not. I watch him for a moment before I dangle the bracelet in front of him. It sparkles and sends a shower of glitter across his forehead and makes him squint. It is too silly to be angry. Too immature. Too ridiculous. *True love forever over every single rainbow. XXX S.L. 1978.* I put on a sweet-little-girl voice to recite the statement. He smiles. There is nothing to worry about. A forty-year-old man had a nostalgic moment. A midlife crisis. I lay the gold bracelet down carefully beside his plate. Ivan takes this as permission to dig his thumb into the center of the orange. He urges me to do the same. I dig my thumb into the center of the orange and split it. Usually we eat the segments as we separate them. Today I arrange them on the plate in a circle before I eat them. The catch was fiddly. It would have been very difficult for Ivan to put it on himself. When he has finished eating his orange, I am going to ask him to put it on again. He licks his finger and thumb clean between tearing the segments off.

. . .

I know I am upset: I cannot decide which shoes to wear. It shouldn't be difficult. I make my choices simple. I have the same shoe—loafers, sensible with stitching on the uppers—in a number of colors. Variations on a theme. For months I have been wearing blue. I am a creature of habit. Today I have taken the red ones from their place on the shoe rack. On my left foot, I have the red shoe. On the right I have the blue. I am wondering about the choice of socks. Everything has a domino effect. Change the color of the shoes and the color of the sock has also to be considered. With blue I always wear green. With red, white. There have to be rules.

I am upset about the bracelet. I timed Ivan. It took him seven minutes to put it on, not including the two minutes he took to clean his nails before he started. I think he knew I'd ask him to put the bracelet on again. As if he had been mentally preparing himself from the moment I saw it.

"Put it back on . . ." I said. I touched his hand as I said it, tried to keep my voice apologetic.

"Well, if you insist . . ." he said. He put on a Scottish accent, raised one eyebrow, gave a full smile. Ivan uses his Sean Connery impersonations in times of potential danger. He is a firm believer in using humor to dissipate difficult situations. He flipped the bracelet onto its back and dragged it off the table toward him; it made a light clunking ratchet sound. He kept his eyes on me, gave a small tilt of his head and then a crooked smile and a wink. He has one blue eye and one green eye. He always winks with the green eye, the left one. Lately when he does it, the wrinkles around his eye deepen so much it becomes prunelike. I made him aware of this fact as he wrapped the thing around his wrist and then laid his arm on the table. He ignored me and maneuvered the clasp around into a more accessible position. He focused on the task. He remained calm. I watched alternately his busy fingers and my watch. Seven minutes, and then he punched the air. The right arm. Bracelet intact. "Mission accomplished, Miss Moneypenny."

I object to being Miss Moneypenny. Bond never had sex with Miss Moneypenny. Ivan cleared his throat: it is his way of reminding me I am closer to forty than thirty. Silence. "Seven minutes is a long time," I said. He told me it took him longer when he put the bracelet on the first time. To console me or to alleviate suspicion. He touched my hand as he said it. He made sure to use his left hand.

On my left foot, I have a red shoe. On the right I have a blue. The cat is watching me look at my feet. When my eyes meet his, he gives a plaintive mew, comes forward, quick staccato steps, and butts the toe of the red shoe with his head. George likes feet. He jumps up on the bed beside me, puts his front paws on my legs and offers me his ears to rub. It is our morning ritual: I put my shoes on, he gets his ears rubbed. I always wear shoes. There is always the possibility that I might have to leave in a hurry.

On my left foot, I have the red shoe. On the right I have the blue. If I wear the red shoes, Ivan will know I am upset. I explain this to George as I move him away. I take the red shoe off and replace it with the blue. Ivan is in the kitchen drying up. We smiled at each other after he won his task.

Nothing was said. He began to wash up. I put the peelings into the compost, wiped the table, swept the floor, went to put my shoes on. I can hear his deliberate movements from the sink to the cupboard, stacking the plates, arranging the cutlery.

Seven minutes. Longer when he put it on before. If there was anything to worry about, he would have kept it secret. But either way, even if he did put it on himself in the first place, he allowed himself the time to do it. Made the time to do it. Put the time aside to do it. He wanted those initials, that inscription, that memory, against his skin. I am going to ask him what the "S.L." stands for. If I know her name, maybe I'll feel less upset. I will ask him later. I'll seduce him and then ask him: he is always more open after sex.

The smell is faint, but it is there. The smell of gas.

I want to tell Ivan about the gas, but I know what he'll do. He'll give me a soft sympathetic smile and take me by the shoulders and walk me to the place where the gas meter used to be by the front door, its shape still a dust shadow showing through the white paint. He'll guide me down the passageway and lead me in turn into the bedroom, the treatment room, the bathroom, the living room, the kitchen; there are no gas appliances in any of them. He'll tap the toe of his foot against the floor at the points where once gas pipes were hidden beneath.

I will be made to remember. I watched him remove all the gas pipes. I watched him roll back carpets, rugs and layers of lino. I watched him lift the floorboards. The copper gas pipes were there, oxidized and bright green against the hollow dark and the dust. He cut them out in sections with a small, bright saw. He was methodical, laying the cut sections neatly in a blue canvas bag ready to take out. They made clean, religious, ceremonial-like sounds as they knocked against each other. I wanted to kneel down and line the pipes up so that at least one end of them would be flush. I wanted to ask him if he wouldn't mind cutting the sections to equal length.

Other men had come and taken out the radiators, the boiler, the gas cooker; other men had come and installed the new electric boiler, cooker and storage heaters. Ivan had come to remove the pipes. I followed him from room to room and leaned in the doorways watching him. He pushed up an imaginary sleeve before any new exertion. I liked watching the muscles working in his arms and back as he sawed. I made him cups of tea. He said he never drank coffee. "Neither do I," I said. That was our first shared smile. I liked the fact he took no sugar in his tea.

The last room he did was the bedroom. As he put the cut pipes into the bag, I knelt down and straightened them so one set of ends would be flush. He carried on without saying a word. He passed no puzzled look. He didn't even give me a sarcastic smile. After he had finished cutting all the pipes and I had finished straightening them, he asked me my name. "Stella," he repeated after me. He stayed that night.

Ivan saw me sniffing the air; the giveaway little bobs of my head. George follows us from room to room, weaving between our legs. If I had worn the red shoes, maybe I wouldn't have smelled the gas.

He is late for work. I watch him as he puts on his jacket. The jacket is blue, municipal looking, the logo of the company he works for in blue-and-red stitching on the front pocket, with a larger version emblazoned across the back. The synthetic material makes crinkling and rustling sounds as he puts his arms into the sleeves.

I take stock of his features to check against my well-rehearsed description. The police will need to make an artist's sketch if he goes missing. I have photographs of him, but it is not the same: if you love someone you should be able to build them in your mind's eye.

Every day when he leaves for work I think, "Maybe today he won't come back."

If the police know who Christopher Walken is, I will say Ivan looks like a thinner version. If they don't know who the actor is, I will say: Ivan—thick blond hair, worn longish, with a side parting. Sideburns. He has a tendency not to shave, and there is ginger in his stubble. His right eye is blue; his left eye is green. They have the shape of fish, the sort of fish a child would draw. They are set at a distance where another eye could fit between them. I have measured this with my little finger. Where the fin would be are his smile lines; they run the length of his temples. The skin there is sometimes very dry. His forehead is high and etched with three frown lines, the middle one shorter than the outside two, placed centrally on the vertical but higher to the top line than the bottom. There is also a vertical line that runs up from the bridge of his nose to just above his eyebrows. It intersects with the bottom frown line to make a little cross. This line has appeared during the time we have been together. It is growing. One day I think it will reach his hairline.

He has his mother's eyebrows. I have not met her but I have seen her picture. They are neat enough to seem plucked; the arch is perfectly placed. The test: Run a pencil diagonally from the outer edge of the nostril across the center of the iris of the eye. Where the pencil meets the eyebrow is where the arch should be. The curve of his arch is exactly there.

Overall the shape of his face is more a rectangle than a square. My face is heart shaped. My nose is small. His nose is strong, long, verging on large. There is a bump and the hint of a twist below the bridge. This is not genetic. It didn't reset properly when it was broken (a childhood accident—a book thrown at him in a classroom). The tip is splayed and there is a dent in the middle; it dips neither up nor down. His nostrils are very pronounced as if someone took a long time with a sculpting tool—poking and lifting and smoothing to give height, pinching to round and tuck and tailor. They are as perfect as little shells. They complement his high cheekbones. His jawline is as definite as the sides of a fifty-pence piece. His mouth is wide with full lips. The top lip has a deep valley beneath his nose and the edge of his lips meets his face in a clipped peak; it gives the impression of being drawn around with lip liner. When we first met, I would rub at it to check. His bottom lip is fuller than his top lip. This makes him look vulnerable. This fuller bottom lip, according to my alternative-medicine books, shows a propensity to stomach problems, which has proved true. I monitor his diet. I should be more strict: I shouldn't let him eat oranges—too acidic. His stomach problem is why he is thin. I think of him more as vacuum-molded, the skin pulled tight to his body. Sinewy, not bony. I think of him as strong. His shoulders are broad. When I first saw him I thought:

"Gallant knight."

A man that should be on horseback.

Passionate and strange: his eyes give out a permanent stare that makes him look both wild and mysterious. Like Christopher Walken. It is also a look that makes him seem lonely. He looks like maybe he has seen things he hasn't wanted to.

But he is heavier than he appears. At night when he gets into bed, the mattress dips and I roll toward him. He is always warm to the touch. Since the first time he stayed, he falls asleep with his arms wrapped around me, pulling me close. Sometimes I think he is going to pull me through his skin and inside him. Swallow me up. It is a good feeling. Safe. Even if during the night we separate, there is always some part of us touching: his foot on mine, my leg stretched over his thigh, my fingers on the inside of his elbow, his hand between my legs or holding hands, linking fingers.

I would not tell the police all these things. Except if they asked if I loved him.

Last night he came home in the early hours of the morning. He slept in the living room so as not to wake me. Or so he said. I was awake, waiting for him. I could hear the TV on low. Something with car chases and guns. Screeching brakes and shots; muffled fast-paced voices; the odd explosion; the lick of fire. Cops and robbers. Ivan likes these sorts of films.

If he had slept in the bed with me, then I would have felt the bracelet as he wrapped his arms around me. It is all getting very complicated.

Ivan is at the door, waiting for me to kiss him good-bye and give him the shopping list. He is stroking his right cheek. There is a patch of soft downy hair there that he strokes when there is time to bide or when he is waiting for me. His jacket is making regular shiny nylon noises with the movement and a link of the bracelet keeps peeking out from the sleeve as it rises up his arm. Everything could have been sorted out very quickly if he had come to bed with me last night. Pillow talk. Secrets. Revelations. Apologies. Forgiveness. Kissing. Sex as the darkness turned grainy in the first light.

I enjoy kissing Ivan in the hallway. It is our special place. The place I first saw him, standing in my doorway, the light behind him. He had a presence. Something within him that sang. His energy was good. I can tell these things, as can my mother and sister, Skye. The world seems to like him. The air holds him fast, I think.

He opens the door and the light from the landing skylight falls into the hallway. I give him the shopping list; he tucks it into a pocket without looking at it. The sun is warm on my fingers curled around the back of his neck. He kisses me and then hugs me close. I can feel the edge of the bracelet, the bit with his name on top and initials underneath, digging into my flesh beneath the shoulder blade. I think perhaps it will cut me.

"I love you," I say.

"I love you too," he says.

I follow him out onto the landing and watch him go down the first flight of stairs, listen to him as he descends the next three flights to the ground floor. He takes the stairs fast, on the inside, his white hand on the oak banister sliding and squeaking all the way down. The floor at the bottom is tiled with black and white squares. Ten steps to the main front door. I can hear him opening it.

"What time will you be home?" I call out.

"Seven."

I usually ask him this before he leaves the flat. I go inside and close the door, worrying if the neighbors have over-heard. If they have overheard, they will think I am treating him like a child. I take the key from my pocket and double-lock the door.

I can still taste his kiss in my mouth. Underneath the sweet bitterness of the orange, there is something cold and flat. Something metallic. I shiver although it is warm. "S.L." I imagine she is blond. Silvery ash blond and petite. "S.L." has a silveriness about it. Ivan's hair is also blond. He has started to go gray at the temples. They must have made a perfect couple to look at. I bet her shoulder tucked neatly into the pit of his arm when they walked side by side. His arm draped across the back of her neck, his large hand protectively enclosing her other shoulder. I bet he would turn from time to time and nuzzle his nose into her sweet-smelling hair. Breathe into it. I have never walked down a street with Ivan. I don't know how we would fit walking side by side in the street. If he prefers to walk on the inside or on the outside of the pavement. If he has a tendency to lean into me or me into him. If he veers to the right or the left or walks straight ahead.

Ivan is gone but his presence lingers. It is like that every day after he leaves. Bits of him still here waiting to catch him up. It will last until twelve o'clock, and then I will begin to miss him.

I move down the passageway to the treatment room and fill a glass with water and rinse my mouth three times.

The treatment room is four meters by five. Its walls are a soft white. The floor pale wood. There is one sash window at its far end; a silver chime hangs within its frame. The chime moves gently in the breeze, its notes high and delicate. I installed a small fan in the window frame to simulate a breeze for when it is too cold to open the window or if the weather is still: the chime is always moving. A curtain of white muslin hangs in front of the window; it keeps the light diffused and billows in from time to time, as was intended. The room faces southwest. At sunset it fills with golden light and shadows. In front of the window is the massage table. It is placed so I can move all around it without restriction. Sometimes the curtain billows in so far its bottom edge skims the body of the woman lying on the massage table. The response varies: a full-bodied shocked twitch to a pleasured sigh; it is a good indicator of how relaxed they are—or are not.

On the adjacent wall, right of the window, is a small wood-and-glass cabinet; it measures one meter square. Its depth is ten centimeters. Ivan made it for me to my instruction. In it are stored the perfumed oils. I get them all from one supplier; their shape, size and color are identical. Dark green glass with white labels. Their names in twelve-point, black Helvetica type. They are arranged in alphabetical order; I make sure to turn all the labels to the front and line them up after I have used them so their names are exactly central. Below the cabinet is the wooden trolley that serves as my mixing table. Two blue-glass bottles stand upon it. One of sweet almond oil, one of grapeseed. Next to them is a small tower of stainless-steel bowls. On the lower level of the trolley I keep the roll of paper to line the massage table. To the right of the trolley is a sink. A movement of the elbow onto a silver lever turns on the single faucet. I wash my hands before and after I touch anyone. Above the sink is a mirror. Today I look tired.

On the other wall adjacent to the window is a tall narrow cupboard. One side is filled with white towels stacked according to their varying sizes in descending order. The other side houses my white shirt-coats. Not so much doctor, more beautician. Slightly tailored. Darts for the bust. One hundred percent cotton; I have a fresh one for each day. On Sundays I wash, starch and iron them while they are still damp.

These things are important; they make the patients feel safe. I should really call them "clients," but to me anyone who needs healing is a patient. Underneath the white coat I wear a white vest and white cotton trousers ironed with a crease down the front.

The room smells of lavender, which I burn to keep the room welcoming. It has uplifting properties; nearly all the women who come to see me seem to be depressed.

When my clients arrive there is a folding Chinese screen behind which they can undress, a towel waiting for them on the heated radiator. A chair on which to sit to take off their shoes. A hook and coat hanger on which to deposit their clothes. I leave them alone in the room until I hear the slight creak of the massage table as they lie upon it. Before entering, I ask if they are ready. Dignity keeps people comfortable. Especially when nearly naked. In exchange I hope their underwear is clean and good, ideally matching. I hope they have recently showered or bathed, at the very least washed their feet. Topped and tailed. These are the sorts of things I would do if it were the other way around. If they haven't made these considerations on their first appointment they will do so on their second and thereafter. I think my face shows disapproval easily.

There are three pictures in the room. A photograph of a waterfall on the wall at the foot end of the table. On the left wall, two reflexology charts. One for the hands. One for the feet.

The diffused light is flattering to the bodies and faces of the women. This is intentional. It makes them feel better about themselves; it is all part of the treatment.

It would be a very peaceful room to die in. That is what Ivan always says. Sometimes we come in here at sunset and drink tea in the golden light. He would like to make love on the massage table. A kiss is as much as I will allow.

There is a silver filing cabinet. A small round table serves as my desk. On it are my appointment book, a bottle of mineral water, two glasses, a box of tissues, a pencil and an eraser.

I check my appointment book. I see four clients a day. Two in the morning at 10:00 and 11:30. An hour for lunch between 1:00 and 2:00. Another client at 2:00. At 3:30 I have tea. My last client at 4:00. An hour and a quarter for each client. Fifteen minutes to prepare for the next. I like to keep to the times. Mrs. Philips is my first client. I keep to the use of second names even if they introduce themselves by their first name: it maintains the necessary distance. I am Ms. Lewis. Always. I don't have my initials on my card. It would invite the question of what it stood for. Women are like that. I am like that.

Mrs. Jones, Ms. Wells and Miss de Wolf are my other clients today. They all know each other; I have been recommended by word of mouth. I am told I am discussed at their dinner parties. They say I am a natural healer. That it is nothing to do with the oils. It's just my hands on them that make the difference. They have discussed my hands: always warm, fingernails short and well manicured, two coats of clear varnish. That my touch is firm. They have noted my white coat is perfectly ironed and starched. I know when their dinner parties are. The day after I get phone calls requesting appointments.

Mrs. Philips is due. I get out her file. I lay out a fresh piece of paper on the bed. I put on my white coat. I walk down the passageway and close all the doors to the other rooms. They will look if they can. There is furniture to identify status but no ornamentation except the effigies of little Japanese cats. I have one placed in the left-hand corner of each room. Little white plaster cats with big black pantomime eyes, sitting on their haunches, their left paws raised by their heads. They are money cats; the left-hand corner is the wealth corner. I charge fifty pounds an hour. The clients do not complain. They say it is worth every penny.

I move down the passageway toward the front door. My rucksack is not tucked into the corner as neatly as it usually is. I push at it with my foot. I notice one of the small side zip pockets is open when it shouldn't be. Kneeling down, I search it with my fingers. My Swiss Army knife is still there. There is something else: a tiny piece of white tissue paper wrapped into a neat parcel. I unfold it. A pale pink disk. About a centimeter and a half across. Imperfect. Old. The edges blunted and chipped. There are raised words on one surface in slightly faded red capital letters: BE MINE FOREVER. A Loveheart sweet. I stare at it. I touch the words with the tip of my tongue. It tastes dusty. The pink fizzes slightly. The red dissolves.

The doorbell rings and Mrs. Philips announces herself on the intercom. I rewrap the sweet in the tissue paper and put it back with the knife in the side pocket and fasten it. I lock George, who has been sitting beside me throughout the proceedings, in the kitchen, retie my hair and button up my white coat to the top. I unlock the door and then double-lock it once Mrs. Philips has entered. "Can you smell gas, Mrs. Philips?" I ask her as I walk in front of her to the treatment room. I hear her sniff the air. "No, Ms. Lewis, I cannot."

Sally, God forbid. Sue. Sheba—Ivan is a quarter Jewish. Sarah; she was blond, too. Siobhan, an Irish girl with freckles.

Sally
Sue
Sheba
Sarah
Siobhan

The list moves continually in my head. Spelled out. Lit up. Faces attached. A hand gesture here. A smile there. It is none of these. But these are the *S*'s I have known. These are my database.

I watch my hands glide up Mrs. Philips's back. Mrs. Philips sleeps. She is a large woman. Not fat. Large. She fills the width of the massage table. I could fit into her twice. Her lingerie is expensive: emerald green silk trimmed with ivory ribbons, bows and lace. Her skin is the color of golden honey. It is a St Tropez. Fake, she reassured me apologetically. She is a clean one; she comes smelling of soap and perfume. Now she smells of cedarwood and sandalwood. Rich and sweet. The smell of fresh pencil shavings. The flesh on her back ripples in even folds. On her fingers she wears gold rings encrusted with diamonds. When her hands move flecks of light move across the walls of the room like shoals of tropical fish. Today on her form she ticked: "Absentminded," "Anxiety," "Lethargy," "Scattered Thoughts," "Worry About the Future," "Tired." I anointed her with the oils and she was asleep within minutes. My clients divide equally between those who sleep and those who talk. I prefer those who sleep. For those who talk, I refrain from being drawn in: conversation only leads to questions. Some fall silent without the engagement, their sentences left unfinished and self-conscious, lost in the tinkling of the chime, which seems to grow louder, more insistent. Others pay no heed; they continue to talk, no hesitation between the sentences, no need for a response. The only time my ears twitch: the subject of clothes, the mention of illicit sex.

Mrs. Philips is having an affair with Mrs. Jones's husband. Two of the talkers have mentioned it, observing her frequent unavailability to lunch. Her new haircut. Her attention to details previously unattended. Painted nails. Reshaped eyebrows. Waxing of the leg higher than the knee. Bikini waxes, they speculate. The St Tropez? I know why Mrs. Philips filled in the questionnaire the way she did.

I never ask my clients how they are feeling. The questionnaire enables a diagnosis to be made without a word being passed. I keep the pencils sharp. On the questionnaire Mrs. Philips circled "25 percent" in the section where she had to state how much better she is feeling than she did the last time we met.

I have booked Mrs. Jones in directly after Mrs. Philips. I consider it part of the treatment; I have seen Mrs. Philips's pencil hover over the box marked "Feelings of Guilt." For two months it has hovered. It will do her good to see Mrs. Jones face-to-face. Before Ms. Ackermann told me about the affair I was more generous. I added juniper to the mix. It is good for alleviating feelings of guilt. And I told her to buy some ylang-ylang, without telling her specifically why. Apparently Mrs. Jones suspects the liaison between Mrs. Philips and her husband. This is what Miss de Wolf said but there has been no confrontation as yet. I should get Ivan to fill in a form and see if his pencil hovers over the box marked "Feelings of Guilt."

Sally
Sarah
Sheba
Shirley
Siobhan
Sue
Suzannah

The least I can do is put it in alphabetical order. It does not console me that my initials are the same. S.L. It occurs to me she may not be blond. She may be a redhead, like me. Maybe I am just her simulator. Her simulacrum. It does not last: strands of silver blond grow through the red mop. Her face is still unseen. Except her eyes. Which I know must be green. Ivan has stated his preference. There are reasons for preferences. Emerald green, like Mrs. Philips's lingerie. But translucent. Full of light. Watery. Dewy. Perpetually seeming on the verge of tears. Ivan finds this moment in me attractive. Attractive beyond concern for the cause. Kissing each welling eye instead of asking me what is wrong.

Mrs. Philips snores. The list of *S*'s rolls in my head. The chime plays on a single repeated note as if to guide me in my internal chant. Her eyelashes would be long and fair and perfectly curled. Her eyelashes would be long and dark and perfectly curled. Her mascara would never run.

It is time to wake Mrs. Philips. I call her name three times. She wakes slowly and raises her head. Her eye makeup has smudged. There is a small dribble of spit on her lower lip and chin. The imprint of the hole she has been resting her face in is a distinct oval, making a smaller face within her own. Her hair is ruffled but largely intact. She licks her lips as she turns onto her side and slides off the bed and wipes her chin. She smiles. "Thank you," she says. I leave the room so she can dress.

I wait on the chair in the passageway. There is a spot of sunlight from the skylight on the Persian rug on the middle of the floor; it is eleven o'clock. It is eight hours until Ivan comes home. I think about the passion with which Ivan and I used to ricochet off the walls, fingers as busy as ants, dismantling clothes, not always making it to the bedroom, collapsing together on the Persian rug. George watching us bemused or running circles around us, the tiny peal of the

23

three bells on his collar punctuating our sighs and groans. Afterward I would hold on to Ivan's little fingers. In a book about sexual energy it said this stops the man losing his vitality.

Now I make sure we have sex at least three times a week. He is always keen. His pleasure is my pleasure.

The smell of gas is less than it was. But it is still there.

Mrs. Philips emerges from the treatment room, dressed, a check in her hand, smiling as the doorbell rings. "That'll be Mrs. Jones," I say. There's the slightest movement at the corner of her eyes. The pursing of two fine lines into one. I simultaneously let Mrs. Philips out and buzz Mrs. Jones in. I follow Mrs. Philips out onto the landing, watch her descend the first flight of stairs, hand on banister, turn to the next flight and disappear from my sight. At the second floor I hear a small dance ensue. Mrs. Philips capitulates, moves around Mrs. Jones. I can tell by the heels. There is the faintest of exchange. They do not stop to talk. They are both still moving. One up, the other down. They talk to the air in front of them. Mrs. Jones talks first. "How are you?" "Fine, and you?" "Well—you know. . . ." Mrs. Philips lets the ambiguity drift. As she opens the main front door, she calls out, "Let's have lunch sometime?" She does not turn as she says it. She could be making the invitation to any passerby in the street. "Yes—let's. . . ." replies Mrs. Jones, who is now facing me. She looks exhausted, but her makeup is immaculately applied and she too has had a haircut. I imagine she instructed the hairdresser for a style that would make her look younger. The color has been taken a shade lighter. It is now a strawberry blond. The style: a purposeful feathery scruff. I have seen pictures of Meg Ryan with the same haircut on the covers of magazines.

On her form Mrs. Jones ticks "Anger," "Bitterness," "Hopelessness," "Insecurity," "Loneliness," "Lack of Self-Esteem" and "Suspiciousness." In the box marked remedy, I write: "Ylang-Ylang, Orange, Geranium, Lemon."

Mrs. Jones wears lingerie the same style as Mrs. Philips's. Both sets, I assume, gifts from Mr. Jones. Mrs. Jones's is a pale canary yellow. I think: yellow is the color of jealousy; canaries are treasured for their song and their ability to die quickly on exposure to gas. I think: I will take to wearing yellow permanently as widows wear black. I shall learn to sing. But yellow is not a color becoming to me; it clashes with my hair and the pink tones of my skin. I restrict my wardrobe to shades of brown.

Gas is yellow. The color of fear. Of anger. Jealousy. Discord.

Maybe her name is Saffron.

Sabella, Sabine, Sabrina, Sadie, Sally, Samantha, Sandra, Sara, Sarah, Sasha, Saskia, Scarlett, Selima, Selina, Seraphina, Seran, Sharon, Sheena, Sherry, Shirley, Shona, Shula, Silvia, Simone, Sindy, Siobhan, Sophie, Sorcha, Stacey, Stella, Stephanie, Susan, Suzanne, Sybil:

The Internet search was useful.

I go with my list of names into the kitchen. George is curled on a pillow on a chair. His ears flatten as I crumple the printout of the names into a ball. As I burn it in the kitchen sink, he opens an eye, gives the slightest twitch of his tail, stretches a front paw, yawns, resumes his position: he is familiar with my burnings.

The paper blackens and curls. The flames tighten, move toward the center. It is how I imagine the earth will be eaten one day. Ivan and George and I holding on to the last, on top of a green hill in a barren landscape.

The names still show. Blacker against black. I run the cold tap and the paper hisses, collapses, disintegrates. Small deaths. The smell of carbon lingers.

I open the French doors from the kitchen onto the balcony. Only a railing and a small gap separate the balcony of the adjacent flat to the right. On my neighbor's balcony, a table and two chairs have been set out and pots of geraniums mixed with lobelia. She has worked fast for someone who has just moved in. I myself favor nasturtiums. Below, the tree-lined street is quiet. I see Ms. Wells, my two o'clock, make her way up the street. She walks quickly, checking her watch, checking her reflection in the windows of the parked cars. She is one house away. As I close the French doors I notice it. Higher than my head height within the top pane, a small white envelope taped to the outside of the glass addressed in a fast fluid script: "To the Cat Owner." The tape runs along each edge, the air bubbles rubbed down with a fingernail.

The knife slipped and cut the tip of my thumb. The pain is delicate. In the space of the next few hours or days, each one of my fingers on each of my hands will gain a flesh wound. It is a phenomenon I have frequently observed: cut one finger and the rest will follow. As I pried off the tape, the knife slipped and the tip of my thumb was cut. It was a paring knife, one of the ones Ivan and I use for our daily oranges. I was impatient; I only had the time that Ms. Wells was undressing. At least the knife is sharp, the cut clean.

Dear Cat-Owner,
   I recently moved in next door, and the room with the balcony is my bedroom. Your cat spends a lot of its night on my balcony, and its bells wake me and keep me awake. I wonder if I could persuade you to take them off, please. My husband says they also keep him awake if he is awake.
   Many thanks,
   C. Heksa

Where the tape was is now a square of glue. The envelope has not been sealed; Mrs. Heksa must be a woman that recycles. A woman with concern for the future of the planet. It is a plus factor against her bloody cheek. It takes two plasters to stop the bleeding.

On her form Ms. Wells has ticked only one box: "Dreams, Recurrent." It is the same box she has ticked for three weeks. Her percentages of how much better she is from one visit to the next have increased gradually but remain low. I ask her if she will write the dream for me. I add it may help. "Perhaps," she says after a while, not making any eye contact. Obviously there is a lot of sex in it. I mix clary sage with rosemary. Her skin is cold under my fingers. She sighs as I press on her kidneys: this is where dreams reside.

I imagine Mrs. Heksa is a woman like Ms. Wells; a woman who dresses in shades of midtone gray to white, a woman with no need for makeup or jewelry, favoring simple sports underwear in black cotton. A concern for the breathing gusset. Breast support without underwire. A haircut that requires no blow-drying. Ms. Wells is quiet, vain, self-assured. Sometimes I think she comes only to take the chance to display her exquisitely toned body. She is an anatomy lesson, a body that even naked would never look nude. She keeps her eyes closed throughout the treatment. They glisten slightly with what I think is antiwrinkle eye-contour cream. It surprises me she dreams at all. There is not a thread of passion in her. There is as much life in her as in a Formica countertop. Sometimes this is how I imagine my other clients see me.

Dear Mrs. Heksa,

Thank you for your letter regarding my cat's bells.

My cat was one of a litter of five. The first time I saw him it was as if he was expecting me. It was a soul thing. As if our meeting was preordained. If you can understand such things. I walked into the room where he and his siblings suckled on their mother in a row and he turned to catch my eye. He was the one in the middle, the only one of the five who turned to look. He was no longer kitten, not quite yet cat. As I touched him he stood and leaned the weight of his small body into my palm. Like an offering. He made a noise from deep in the back of his throat. Half growl. Half drawl. Primordial. It went to the core of me. It aroused something pure. A look ran between us that entered the realm of the eternal.

I had not gone to choose a cat. I had been simply visiting. But we found each other. We are devoted to each other. I can describe the texture of his fur at every different part of his body. I know how his markings begin and end. We have many pure moments. My cat was a sign, a reward: he came into my life on the very day I threw out every single photograph in my possession. All my past gone. I trust you will understand it is very important to me that I know where he is at all times. The bells allow this to be the case. Hearing them reassures me. Of something beyond the cat itself. His bells wake me and keep me awake.

I hope you have settled into your new home.

Yours sincerely,

Ms. Lewis

I made sure not to mention his name. She may use it.

I will not write this letter. I will not write any letter. My mind has run the gauntlet of impossible tempers induced by lack of sleep and the long drop from the balcony. Murder. Yellow police tape. Matted fur. I will remove the three bells from his collar. The alternative: to seal up the cat flap, keep him in. I have already done him the injustice of removing his sex. Even without the possibility of tempers, there is the possibility of a knock on the door. Arguments. Court injunctions.

If I keep the bells on, Mrs. Heksa may take to the use of barbed wire.

Skye and her three daughters have arrived, a swath of floral-print sundresses; the girls in flip-flops, Skye in sling-back high-heeled sandals. They weave around Ms. Wells in her neutral grays on the landing. Ms. Wells looks like a dead tree in summer.

The three silver bells chime with labored rhythm; one now hangs on a piece of ribbon around each of my nieces' necks. They are trailing string up and down the passageway, playing with George. Their girly laughter intermittently fills the kitchen; George paws after them frantically.

"How is Ivan?" There is a gap where there should be an *I* in "Ivan." Like somebody trying to reach a high note and not getting there.

I tell Skye about the bracelet and the sweet folded in tissue paper. She leans close. "Gosh." She touches her cheek as she says it. Old-fashioned words. She crosses and recrosses her legs, smooths down the skirt of her dress where it has ridden up over her knees. Where did she learn to act like this? Definitely not from our mother. Although she has our mother's knees.

She lights one of her French unfiltered cigarettes and inhales deeply. She kicks off her sling-back high-heeled sandals.

"What're you going to do?" she coos as she puts the spent match into the ashtray and exhales.

"You may have to follow him for me."

I have realized it may have come to this. Following Ivan. To be sure about things.

Skye's gaze moves across the table to the floor. She is holding off a smile.

"Seriously?" she says.

"Seriously," I say.

She will do it if I ask her: she is my big sister.

She takes another drag on her cigarette and exhales.

I watch the miasma thicken, then plume as it drifts toward the passageway; I usher her onto the balcony and close the door. She is not supposed to smoke inside the flat: it makes the gas smell stronger. There is also the danger of explosion. She sits the way she does when defiant. I know it well, the pose. Feet up on the edge of the balcony table. Chair pushed back enough to allow for this. A stiffness in her upper back. There is a small trail of ash on the balcony floor beside her where she has missed the ashtray. Cigarettes are a relatively recent addition to her life: a year since she and Tim parted. She smokes too much.

Skye and her three daughters posed on a sofa, a vase of flowers to the right, a mirror behind them so you can see the backs of their heads. Ivan has scaled it up to letter size from the photograph: an exact copy in pencil. It is hard to discern it is a drawing. It is photorealistic. I see no point in copying a photograph exactly. It seems redundant but Ivan is reluctant to draw from life.

"He's good, isn't he?"

They look from the photo to the drawing and back. They all have thick, curly black hair, worn short. They all have the same-shaped faces. The same-shaped noses. The same pouty mouths. I am grateful the girls have only taken after Skye.

"It's brilliant."

"I suppose."

I watch them in their floral prints admiring their likeness. It's like watching an Eric Rohmer film. They should be speaking French.

I look at the square of tape glue left on the windowpane. I think: Mrs. Heksa has long legs if she climbed the gap between the balconies with ease. I speculate reasons she did not just leave the letter in my post-box downstairs or outside my front door; perhaps she is making a point about trespassing. My cat on her balcony, she on mine.

I reread the letter. I note the *C* could be an unfinished *S*.

Skye bends to pull the sling-backs over her heels. She smiles at me as she straightens up. "Call me when you know more about the bracelet," she says. I think she likes it that at last there is something possibly not good about Ivan. At the front door she instructs her three daughters to kiss their "auntie" good-bye. I kneel down to help them. The youngest is first.

"Good-bye, Lucy."

"Good-bye, Auntie."

"Good-bye, Mia.'

"Good-bye, Auntie."

"Good-bye, Helen."

"Good-bye, Auntie."

"Come on, Mum," they say to Skye as they drag her onto the landing

If I had children they would call me "Mother."

I watch them from the balcony as they walk to Skye's car and get in and drive away.

I watch George playing with his tail on Mrs. Heksa's balcony. When I call to him he comes to me with no hesitation. He makes no sound as he jumps the gap.

Miss de Wolf gives me a conspiratorial smile as she notices in my open diary the back-to-back appointments of Mrs. Philips and Mrs. Jones. "That must have been interesting," she says. I keep my expression unreadable, the corners of my mouth level. My eyes blank. My forehead relaxed. An art learned as a child. Pretending to look dead. When I let her out she turns twice on the stairs to look at me with the same smile. There is satisfaction like a cape across her shoulders. A skip in her footfall down the stairs and across the black and white tiles. She shouts "Bye" as she opens the main front door, loud and overcheerful. It echoes up into the chamber of the stairwell. She waits for me to respond. "Good-bye, Miss de Wolf," I say, my voice without warmth, and she closes the door quietly behind her. I think she thinks I am the lid finally pried off by a screwdriver in a deft hand. Or that I have become part of her gang.

I have reprinted the list of names beginning with *S*. If Ivan doesn't give me the name, I will have to call each one out like a register and watch to see if the pupils of his eyes dilate.

It is seven o'clock. I am waiting for Ivan.

My baby doll is black and sheer and trimmed with marabou feathers.

The bra and pants match.

There are also feather-trimmed kitten-heel slippers.

I'm not one for mixed messages.

I wait in the bedroom, lounging on the bed in a manner I have seen in films, magazines, commercials advertising lingerie and paintings of courtesans. On my right side, leaning on my right elbow, head rested in the palm of my right hand, left hand draped across my right thigh. Left leg slightly farther forward and bent at the knee so the toe of the kitten-heel slipper on my left foot lies upon my right calf. In films the pose signifies the imminent promise of sex. Or murder. Or both. I know I am perfectly framed within the bedroom doorway.

Underneath the bed, within easy reach, is my list of names beginning with *S* and the Loveheart sweet wrapped in tissue paper. I smell of rose, the room of jasmine. Heavy dub reggae climbs the walls and thickens the air. My back will be to him when he walks into the room. He likes the nape of my neck and the peach of my bottom. When he walks into the room I will stay still for a moment and then turn my head slowly toward him and offer him an easy eye. But no smile. And then turn back. That is all it will take.

Rose and jasmine; it is a good mix. Heady. Syrupy. Both are aphrodisiacs.

I am cleanly shaved. A question: should I insist that he be likewise? No. It would take too long.

The marabou feathers sway as they measure my breath.

When Ivan lies down beside me and kisses the back of my neck I will turn over and face him. I will smile and undress him. I will strip him naked except for the bracelet. And he will keep his eyes closed as he always does. After I have kissed his nipples, allowed equal attention to both, I will straddle him: this position offers him quick satisfaction, one hand on my breast, the other resting on my waist. The foreplay is my pose. My marabou feathers and kitten heels. And then as he dozes beneath me I will run my finger along the bracelet, the flat bit, the bit where his name is written, and with my head cocked to one side I will ask coquettishly, "The initials on the back—what does the *S* stand for?" I will have to use the index finger of my left hand. The index finger of my right hand has become twinned with its thumb. A plaster wrapped around its tip. I caught it in the grater while grating the Parmesan. In the kitchen the table is prepared for supper, and on the stove a pan of water is ready for boiling. Ivan is bringing home fresh ricotta-and-spinach tortellini, charcoal-grilled artichokes marinated in herbs and olive oil. I have already toasted the pine nuts. There is a small green salad in the fridge. Before we met, Ivan never ate anything Italian. He still views pizza as expensive cheese on toast with tomato for extra. He is keener on Chinese. He says the day I go out (he imagines wrongly I want to go out), he will take me to a place where they cut carrot slices in the shape of butterflies. When I slice carrots I count the slices as I go. An average medium-size carrot sliced on the diagonal equals twelve to fifteen slices.

Ivan is coming up the stairs. I count the steps as he takes them. There are twenty between each floor. He has brought home his tool kit. I can hear the hollow rattle of metal against metal as it bangs against his thigh as he takes the steps. On the side of his right thigh just above the level of his knee there is always a bruise. In a moment I will see it and run my hand over it.

It is more difficult than I anticipated, undoing the buttons of his shirt. He holds my wrists and observes the plasters.

"What happened?" he asks.

I smile it off. Domestic details could ruin the mood. I could fall into the sympathy he offers.

"Nothing—a little scratch."

His nipples taste of salt.

He is excited, I can tell. He touches me as if he is handling hot eggs. I kneel over him and his eyes close and his hands find their positions, waist and breast, as if they are going home.

I use the rhythm of the music to guide me. It takes less than one track. It takes a verse and a chorus. His breath quickens and calms. He puts his arms around me and draws me close. His breath grows even. I wait another track and pull away to lie beside him. I hold his left hand across my stomach with my right hand. I stroke the bracelet with my left index finger.

"Ivan."

He is nearly asleep. I lean on my elbow and lean over his face. I concentrate on his lips.

"Ivan—sweetie—what does the *S* stand for?"

A short nasal hum is his response.

"The *S*—what does it stand for?"

The tip of his tongue appears and moves cautiously over the full oval of his lips and disappears again. He bites his bottom lip and releases it. He takes an in-breath.

The out-breath of her name divides into three.

"SO–PHI–A."

The shape her name makes on his lips. A kiss. A smile. Wonderment.

He opens his eyes. They are milked. There is no glimmer. No depth of color in the blue or in the green. I cannot see myself contained perfectly in the black of his pupils. She has swum into them. It is not quite sadness, the look. More a look as if he has suddenly remembered what he has forgotten. A lost look. Distant. And then it is gone and he offers me, "*L* is for Lawrence—the *S* stands for Sophia, the *L* for Lawrence." The Scottish accent crept back in.

"Sophia Lawrence." Her hair moves from blond to brown and back. I smile: he has given me the information I wanted. He has had all day to prepare. He probably thinks the sex is a bonus lying somewhere between bribe and reward. He closes his eyes again and finds my shoulder with his head, which I kiss. I want to ask what color her hair is.

I tell him as I get up: "Food will be ready in ten minutes," and he gives me a thumbs-up.

Sophia. Very similar in sound to Sulfur. Yellow, as I suspected.

Sophia Lawrence.

I put the pasta into the boiling water. I put the green salad onto the table, pour the artichokes into a pale green bowl, scoop the pine nuts into a pale blue bowl. I pour two glasses of water.

Sophia Lawrence.

I open the balcony doors. The evening is balmy. It feels Continental. Italian.

Sophia Lawrence: her mother no doubt a fan of Sophia Loren.

Maybe her hair is brown. Her eyes large and hazel.

Maybe Ivan is lying. Perhaps he is teasing me. Was going to say "Loren" and changed his mind.

I call Ivan as I drain the pasta. He arrives in boxer shorts, carrying George, wanting to know what has happened to George's three bells. I read him the letter as he washes his hands.

"Better than him being thrown off the balcony," he says.

"Exactly," I say.

These are the good bits. The bits where we move along the same lines of thought.

I serve him eight more pieces of pasta than me. I sprinkle some pine nuts on top, as suggested in the recipe.

George sits on the chair between us. His face just visible

above the table. He watches the bracelet move up and down Ivan's arm. I watch the bracelet move up and down Ivan's arm. It will bruise the bone on his wrist, and I will have to rub it with arnica cream. It will be Sophia's bruise.

"What color is her hair?"

Ivan looks at me. He points at his mouth with his fork. He knows I don't like it if he talks with his mouth full. I wait for him to swallow.

"Whose?" he says.

"Hers." I touch the bracelet. I cannot bring myself to say her name out loud. It catches somewhere in my chest.

"Blond," he says.

"Natural?"

Ivan shrugs.

"What sort of blond?"

There is no response.

"Strawberry blond, honey blond, Helsinki blond, ash blond, Arctic blond, platinum blond?" I punctuate using the fork on the edge of my plate.

Ivan looks as if he is thinking about it. "Blond blond," he says finally.

He chews the last piece of his tortellini. For the sake of his stomach, I have told him each bit of food put in his mouth has to be chewed forty times. He often tells me how much better his stomach is since he's been living with me. I count with him in my head. He swallows, pushes his plate away and picks at the pine nuts remaining in the bowl. He scrutinizes one close up.

"Like your hair is copper, her hair was blond. The last 39

time I saw her was July twelfth, 1978 at four P.M., after school, outside the school gates. She was going away. She gave me the bracelet then, and the sweet. The one you found. The one under the bed with the list of names."

He smiles at me.

"Twenty-four years ago, that was the last time you saw her?"

"Twenty-four years ago," Ivan repeats.

He eats the pine nut and the bracelet falls to halfway down his arm. One half of his mouth smiles as he leans across the table and fingers the marabou trim on my baby doll, gazing at me, both mocking and sympathetic. His thumb slides across my collarbone. He walks his fingers up my neck. I know what he is going to do and I let him. He flicks my earlobe.

"Ah, my little Moneypenny. Now you know."

I wrap my hand gently around the bracelet.

"Where did she go?" I ask.

"Canada," he says.

"Canada," I repeat after him.

I take a sip of water; I think of geese and how it seems right that a silver blonde goes to Canada. A land I associate with snow and mountains. I take another sip of water; I think how geese migrate back and forth.

"Did she ever come back?"

Ivan strokes my cheek. "Not that I know of." The Scottish accent. A Sean Connery look. A half smile on his face. He stands up, begins to clear the dishes.

"I'm going to wash up now," he says.

It is the deal. He shops. I cook. He washes up. I dry.

Ivan sleeps and Sophia sleeps beside him. The space between us filled with her as I asked him questions. I have learned her eyes are green. As I had thought. Their lashes so fair as to be almost transparent. Her eyebrows the same. Her nose is aquiline. Her mouth only a change in color upon her face. The lips not full but flush and fine. She is slim. Her hips narrow. Her legs long. Arms delicate. Hands small. The moons on her fingernails high. She is the one who broke his nose. She threw her shoe at him. I asked him what sort of shoes she wore. What sort of clothes. He said she wore all sorts of shoes. He said this with particular emphasis. He said she was fond of clothes made of light material, silk and fine cotton, clothes that caught the breeze as she walked and pressed and found her slender body, outlining its subtle curves.

I am wearing the bracelet now. The Loveheart sweet has been returned to its home.

As Ivan got into bed I took the sweet from under the bed and unfolded it from its tissue paper. I pushed it against his lips.

"You should eat it," I said.

"No," he said, and he took the sweet from me, and put it on the table on his side of the bed.

I got into the bed, lay right on the edge of my side of the mattress, as far as I could from him, but decided this was not a good idea if I wanted answers. I moved so there was a distance between us down the center of the bed. Cool but not cold. I was casual.

"Where have you been keeping them all this time, the trinkets?"

He told me he had kept them in his cigar box, in the lockup, in the garage underneath the flats.

His belongings when he moved in with me: a black bin liner half full of clothes, an old cigar box of "personal possessions." The bag I unpacked into the third drawer down of the chest in the bedroom. But the cigar box I would not allow to stay in the flat. I had a condition. No items that would invite questions about the past. Nothing that would provoke inquiry. Information on a voluntary basis only. He has been good until now.

"Why did you put on the bracelet?" My voice soft, leaning toward sympathy.

He saw a girl in the street who resembled her. That is what he told me. It made him remember. He opened his cigar box and he took from it the sweet and the bracelet. He had meant to take the bracelet off again. He had forgotten.

"Sorry," he said. He ran his hand along my arm. "Would you like to see the other things?"

He squeezed my shoulder. He wanted me to see the other things.

"Okay," I said, and he left the flat and went to the lockup

and returned with the cigar box under his arm. He was out of breath. He had been running. He couldn': wait. He sat beside me on the bed, knees bent, cigar box centrally placed between his feet.

"Are you sure?"

I nodded my head. Tried to smile. I sat up to show my interest.

I think he would have shown me even if I had said "no."

The lid lurched to the right as he lifted it: the left hinge was broken, the right hinge squeaking as if it needed oiling. Inside, three objects of different shape and size, each wrapped in the same tissue paper as the sweet. He took them out, laid them on the bed between us. I could see that still in the box was an old passport, its corner edge clipped. Peeking out from underneath its edge, the photograph of his mother, the one I have seen, the one that shows he has inherited her perfect eyebrows. He saw me looking and he closed the lid.

He lifted the shape that was long and bulky, placed it on his thigh and unwrapped it. He held it up for me to see; it was a plait of hair. "From when she had had her first big haircut. Waist to just below the shoulder," he said; he turned and marked the same places on my body with the side of his hand in a chopping motion. The plait was silver-white more than blond. It had not lost its luster. I didn't want to touch it. I don't think he wanted me to touch it, the way he put it down on the bed, on his right side, out of my reach.

Next he unwrapped a black-and-white passport-size picture. He held it in the palm of his hand to show me. Ivan and

Sophia, side on. Her hair and his hand obscuring her face, but discernible is the fact they are kissing. On the back a date: May 1977. I saw this as he put it facedown on the pillow. He handed me the last item, told me to unwrap it. Underneath the tissue was a small folded square of lined paper. I opened it out. There were three tiny drawings in a row. They showed the progression of a heart into a pair of kissing swans.

"Very sweet," I said as I refolded the picture along its creases and handed it back to Ivan but I was thinking: she has turned from goose to swan; swans mate for life; swans die of grief should their partner be taken away. Ivan gave me the slightest raise of his eyebrows, picked up the discarded tissue and carefully rewrapped the picture. He took as much care with the photograph and the plait. I saw him stroke the plait with the back of his index finger before he finally covered it from view. I saw something like electricity run up his face. He laid all the objects side by side on his pillow. I watched as he stretched to reach the sweet on the bedside table; I caught his arm as he straightened up.

"What about the bracelet?"

He smiled at me as he offered me his wrist so that I could undo it. "I thought perhaps you may want to wear it for a while," he said as I struggled with the catch. The bracelet fell with a light thud onto the bed.

"Why would I want to do that?"

He made this gesture with his hand motioning it from his chest to mine. "A sharing thing—what's mine is yours. . . ."

He did not let me answer. He put down the sweet, he took my wrist in one hand, he picked up the bracelet with the other and fastened it around my wrist. I did not resist. I was touched.

"Anything else you need, Miss Moneypenny?"

I shook my head. He picked up the sweet and wrapped it, opened the cigar box. He caught my hand as I reached in to lift out his old passport. Then he seemed to change his mind, his grip loosening. I lifted out the passport, turned the cover.

His hair is longer in the picture, reaching his shoulders, his face fatter, the jawline not so defined. His expression very serious. As if he is waiting for an answer to something important. I turned the page. Two stamps. An entry and an exit. Canada. Date of entry: August 16, 1973. Date of exit: December 18, 1978. I looked up at Ivan.

"They aren't real," he said.

I stared again at the stamps. I thought about how it was possible that he could have forged them but how was I supposed to know? I wanted to rub at them to see if they smudged.

"I'll tell you tomorrow—don't ask me why now—I'm tired."

It was more a plea than an instruction. He took the passport from me, placed it back in the cigar box, placed each of the carefully wrapped items on top of it, closed the lid and put the box in the bedside drawer.

"I love you," he said as he got into bed and curled up beside me. I noticed he had his hand over his stomach.

"Can I get you some fennel tea for your stomach?" I asked him.

"No, I just want to go to sleep now, Stella," he said.

Three million, eight hundred forty-four thousand, nine hundred twenty-eight square miles. The map of Canada spreads over four pages of the world atlas. It is a country I always assume to be on my left. To the west. No matter where I am. The population is 30,287,000. Tonight the population is one. Her name is Sophia. Swaddled in fur, she moves slowly across the snow and ice toward the mountains. Her silver-blond hair lashes in the bitter winds like a fury around her head. Her cheeks have reddened in the cold and her lips have cracked. As she walks, she brings her hands up to either side of her mouth and shouts a name. She turns her head as she says it. It is carried away by the wind. It is Ivan's name she is calling. In the atlas it says the life expectancy of a female in Canada is eighty-one.

I ring Skye from the kitchen.

"Her name is Sophia. She went to live in Canada."

"Wait," she says.

There is silence followed by the scratch of the flint as Skye lights her cigarette. She coughs as she inhales.

"Now, tell me things."

As I talk to Skye I watch the bracelet shift up and down my arm. Already the first bit of sunlight creeps in. It catches on the bracelet and sends its reflection across the wall and ceiling.

WEDNESDAY

Today I wear my red shoes. Today the gas is so thick I can feel it push against my skin; if it stains it will be yellow. Yellow like turmeric. I have opened all the windows. I have laid our oranges on our plates. Poured our glasses of water. To Ivan's glass I add five drops of essence of honeysuckle; it is known to help alleviate yearning for the past. When he leaves I'll strip the bed and wash the sheets. I have filled the washing machine with soap and bleach, set the dial to ninety degrees. The hottest wash to drown her in. It is not the normal day to change the sheets. That is Sunday. On Sundays we also clean the windows. I write "lighter fuel" at the bottom of Ivan's shopping list. In brackets I write "to remove the tape from the balcony door window." It is important always to think ahead. It is also important to explain things.

Ivan looks at my red shoes as he walks into the kitchen.

His smile is swift. Enough to acknowledge the change. There and then gone.

He kisses me on the cheek. We sit down.

"Okay?" I ask.

"Okay," he answers back.

A compliant silence between us. Don't rock the boat in troubled seas. I will not ask him why he forged his passport. It is enough that he did. Not being able to get there, pretending to go there. I will not ask him and he will not tell me. Because he knows I know. Between us run soft smiles and long eye contact. The oranges remain untouched. I want him to drink the water but instead he reaches over and fingers the bracelet on my wrist. He wants to tell me things. I believe it is only kind to help him out.

I ask, "What was she like?"

As if he has rehearsed it, he comes out with, "She was a party girl. She made the most of things. She could never keep still. She always had to go out."

I return the sad smile he has offered me.

I pick up my orange, throw it from palm to palm. Sophia: life and soul of a party. Sophia: the woman who is able to cross roads to get to the other side. Crosses oceans to get to other countries. I watch the orange move from one hand to the other, listen to the cold slap it makes. I am ashamed how meek the competition I offer is. I imagine every wall in every room in the flat take one step forward.

"She sounds like fun."

"She was."

I put the orange down and roll it around the plate. "You must have loved her very much."

Ivan nods his head slowly. It reminds me of a child whom one asks, "Are you lost?" who is unable to answer, the admission too great to contemplate. He takes a sip of his water and then takes my hand in his. "No more than I love you."

He should have said, "I love you more." I understand that this is the deal in these situations.

Maybe if I hadn't worn the red shoes I wouldn't have fallen down the stairs. Maybe if I hadn't asked the next question he wouldn't have stormed out of the kitchen telling me to "Get a life." We struggled by the front door as he tried to unlock it and I tried to stop him. There are five small bruises from his fingertips where he held my arm so tight. There was a moment of playing statues just after he opened the door. His anger pinning me to the spot. I followed him out. I followed him down the stairs. Calling his name. Saying I was sorry. He was a whole landing ahead. At the first-floor landing, in sight of the main front door, I realized how far I had gone and the panic attack came; my heart began to pound, my limbs tremble, my breath stagger in my chest. And then there was the brush of fur against my ankle. George sniffing the stairs beside me, his head bobbing as he increased his pace, smelling new smells as Ivan opened the main front door. I had visions I can't admit to for fear of their coming true. I called out to Ivan, "The cat! The cat!" And as I hesitated to catch George, to stay still or run, I stumbled and fell.

I saw Ivan hurry to close the door and turn to catch the cat.

"Get up," he said, and he handed me George.

Maybe if I hadn't been wearing my red shoes I wouldn't have fallen down the stairs.

All I asked was, "Was she good in bed? Was she better than me?"

I am burning frankincense to help me breathe more evenly and deeply.

10:00 Mrs. Ackermann
11:30 Miss Keithley
2:00 Ms. Teller
4:00 Mrs. Shushan

I check my watch: 9:00. I open the filing cabinet, get their documentation ready. I put on my white coat. Hear the front door being unlocked. I stand in the passageway, wait for the door to open. Wait to see Ivan. Wait for the embrace.

It is Skye.

"I just had a feeling. I just had to be here," she says.

Skye says, "Rock 'n' roll or disco? Or do you fancy a bit of techno?"

She examines my small collection, the "best of" compilations as advertised on TV and ordered via the Internet. Quick and easy. The selection already made. The collection of CDs is arranged by years. It starts at 1950.

52   "You choose," I say. I know she'll choose rock 'n' roll. It

suits her style. Her dress sense. Today she is wearing an original. A vintage piece. More flowers and tight at the waist. She thinks it will do me good to dance. It will get the circulation going. Wake me up. Cheer me up. She shouts this across at me, already anticipating the volume. She brings her arms up in front of her, wrists limp, hands hanging down, like an impersonation of James Cagney, waiting to catch the beat. If it were one of her sporty days, she'd have put on the techno. But the hands would have adopted the same starting pose. She moves toward me, shoulders leading, and takes my hand and drags me from the chair at the same time as the phone on the floor by my feet begins to ring. She picks it up, still dancing.

"Hello, Ms. Lewis's residence. Hello. Hello." She moves the phone away from her ear and pulls a disgruntled face. "Must have been a wrong number."

I had hoped it would be Ivan ringing up to say he was sorry.

Skye makes me dance. She takes my hands and pulls me toward her and then pushes me away, twirls me. And asks me to twirl her. Her skirt grows out to full circle. Any chance to show off her legs.

Skye laughs. "Maybe it was Sophia," she says.

I turn off the rock 'n' roll as punishment. She shouldn't mock me. I have shown her the contents of the cigar box. I have shown her the bruise on my arm where Ivan gripped me.

"You look tired," Skye says as she leaves. She strokes underneath my eyes. "You should get some sleep."

. . .

Mrs. Ackermann has arrived. It is obvious Miss de Wolf has been talking to her. Relating my back-to-back booking between Mrs. Jones and Mrs. Philips. She can't keep the grin from her face. I apologize that today my massage won't be so deep as I've injured my finger and thumb and I hold them in front of her face, hoping sympathy will remove her inquiring expression. It seems to work. On her form she ticks: "Mental Strain from Overwork. "Procrastination." I mix rosemary with sandalwood.

Her inquiring expression seemed to return as I showed her out.

"I hope your hand gets better soon," she said.

"Thank you," I said. It is important to remain polite. I returned her smile and closed the door.

When the phone rang I ran for it. I thought it was Ivan. "Hello."

No one answers.

"Hello?"

Whoever it is hangs up. I put down the phone; it rings again.

"Hello, Ms. Lewis, this is Miss Keithley. I'm ill. It came on this morning. . . ."

"Did you ring before—just now?" I ask her.

"No," she said.

I thank her for her call although I am annoyed: I will be unable to dial 1471 to get a number for the previous caller.

I have rung Ivan.

"Ivan, did you just call?"

"No," he said. He hung up.

He is still angry with me. And my question. My questions.

There is a Sophia Lawrence born in 1859. A Sophia Lawrence born in 1855. Another born in 1858. Another still born in 1825. Still yet another in 1707. There is Sophia Lawrence who is a tennis player in Pepperdine. A Sophia Lawrence who is a statistician and who regularly attends informal meetings of experts on labor-market information and is a specialist in equal opportunities. There is a Sophia Lawrence in a short story by a man called Simon Schwarz. And a Sophia Lawrence who is a will testator in New York. There is a Sophia Lawrence in the directory of the Marine Interests of the Great Lakes, comprising a complete list of all vessels navigating the lakes arranged alphabetically. This Sophia Lawrence is a boat or a ship. There is no Sophia Lawrence listed in Canada. There is no Sophia Lawrence listed in London. This is what the computer tells me.

It is twelve-thirty. It is six and half hours till Ivan comes home. George sleeps peacefully on the kitchen chair. The oranges still remain intact.

The front doorbell rings. Soft knocking follows it. I am not expecting anyone.

Through the peephole a woman in her mid-thirties. Wearing a mauve paisley scarf Gypsy style and dark sunglasses, flat lips glossy with Vaseline. A high-necked white vest. Small gold hoop earrings. I cannot see her hair. It has been tucked in to her scarf.

"Hello?" I ask through the door.

"Hello, are you the cat owner?"

"Yes."

"I just wanted to say thank you for taking off the bells."

"That's okay."

She looks down at the floor. She is waiting for me to open the door. She looks up at the peephole.

"Maybe you'd like to come over for coffee sometime." Her voice has an accent I can't quite place.

"Thank you."

"Good-bye."

"Good-bye."

I watch her turn and move away toward the stairs. Pale-colored Capri trousers, white sandals. She is carrying a basket, emerging from it the tassels of a tartan blanket and the cylindrical shape of a vacuum flask, a book. For a moment I am filled with a longing to sit in a park in the sunshine.

Orange and red and yellow. I am staring at the nasturtiums; I am trying to remember.

I shake out the blanket to lay it on the balcony. It catches the breeze and lifts and sways before it falls; the corners fold in as it settles. I kneel and reach over to straighten and smooth them out.

The sun moves lower in the sky but the light grows white and hot; the bracelet grows warm against my wrist. I think about Sophia and Ivan. I think about blankets and romantic liaison. I think about whether Ivan will ever answer the question "Was she better than me?" There is something I need to remember that I have forgotten. That is not exactly the feeling but it resembles it. Something I cannot place. It does not go away when I fold up the blanket and return it to the cupboard in the hallway.

Ivan's mother, a woman with perfect eyebrows, picks up the phone after five rings. I have never met her. This is the first time I have ever rung her.

"Hello?"

"Hi, it's Stella."

"Yes?"

"Stella, Ivan's girlfriend."

"I know who you are. Is something wrong?"

"No, no. Ivan is fine."

"Thank goodness for that." Her reply is breathy, relieved.

The phone line crackles, a cordless phone, the hum of metal. I do not like cordless phones. You always get interference.

I make my voice low and soft. I make it so I sound hurt. I need information.

"He's been talking about someone called Sophia."

She sighs heavily.

"I don't know what I can tell you, Stella."

"Was she beautiful?"

"So people said."

"People?"

"Everyone. . . . She made heads turn. . . ."

"Tell me what happened."

"It's not my place. . . ."

The phone line crackles and fuzzes as she moves around.

"When you move the line breaks up."

She apologizes. Keeps still.

"I tried to ask Ivan but it seemed to upset him."

"It was a painful time for him," she says.

"Please tell me—it would help me to understand."

She breathes heavily into the phone. "She was only here for a year—family traveled around. And then she left. He was very ill. Heartbroken when she left, so he followed her out to Canada, but she'd met someone else. That is the long and short of it."

The long and short of it: he has lied. The other thought that follows fast behind: he downplayed. To spare me. To spare my feelings.

"Is that so?" I hear myself say.

We are quiet then. I think she is sitting down now; I can hear a change in her breath.

"It was a long time ago, Stella. I can tell you she never made Ivan happy. They seemed to always argue. Not like you two—you make my boy very happy, Stella. Without a shadow of a doubt."

Her voice has grown casual as if she wants to get more familiar, more chatty with me.

She is sipping at something. She thinks this is going to be a long conversation.

"She still sends me Christmas cards . . . on her last card, she wrote she was getting divorced—it didn't surprise me. She was a difficult person."

"Does Ivan know this?"

"Yes, I told him—he wasn't surprised either."

I ask, "Did she say she might come back—back to England?"

"Not that I can remember."

I ask, "Did she have long legs?" Just to be sure.

"Quite long," is the response.

I tell her, "I am sorry I have to go; a client has just arrived."

Her parting words: "It's all water under the bridge."

Already I have looked up the width of the Atlantic.

Already I have speculated as to the whereabouts of Ivan's current passport, the one that is valid and ready to use.

They seemed to be always arguing.
Sophia never made Ivan happy.

I think, "What has happiness got to do with love?"

The question I wanted to ask but didn't.

"On her Christmas cards, does she send her love to Ivan?"

"Does she write, 'Send my love to Ivan'? Does she draw a heart and put a little kiss beside it?"

I take the bracelet off, hold it in my hand until it gets warm. "Was she better than me?"

The thought presented itself like a whisper. *Ivan never had sex with Sophia.*

It came to me as I sat on the edge of the bath and with a small nail file removed the gold plate from the bracelet to reveal the dull silver underneath.

I filed away the gold on a link on the underneath of the bracelet so he won't see.

Hot sticky preludes that came to nothing. In parks. In the backseats of cinemas and cars. In bedrooms, with parents watching TV downstairs or next door. Music on loud to cover up the sighs and creaks of the bed. "But I love you," Ivan says as she curls her hand around his to halt its progress, as she gets up suddenly and sadly shakes her head because he had found his way on top of her.

Sometimes the same scene begins again before the other finishes, like "Frère Jacques" sung in a round.

The insight makes me a little giddy, brings a tightness just below the ribs. With it a slight smile.

He doesn't pick up the phone when I ring him. I leave a message: "I apologize. Please forgive me."

He still hasn't rung back.

My two o'clock is Ms. Teller. I do not like her skin. It's like parchment. When I touch it, I think my fingers may go through her. I imagine they would find organs also made from finest paper that crumble to dust on contact. I gather from the questionnaire she filled in that she has never been loved; I use marjoram for loneliness and tangerine for lack of joy and dry skin. At four I treat Mrs. Shushan, who suffers from recurrent backache; she likes to come late in the day, when the light in the room turns golden. She is also Mrs. Philips's sister-in-law. "She was here earlier, yes?" she asks me. "Mrs. Jones rang me looking for her." I say nothing. I suspect I am being used as an alibi. At six I feed George. When he has finished, he sits on my lap to let me rub his ears. At half past six, I wash my hands and set the table in preparation for Ivan's return and then watch for his van from the balcony. I see Mrs. Heksa turn in to the street. I note the way she walks, sexy, lazy, all in the hips. It is how I imagine Sophia would walk. I move back inside in case she sees me, hear her as she swings her keys as she walks up the path. I wait for her in the passageway, watch her through the peephole as she opens her front door directly opposite mine, notice the backs of her arms are sunburned. In the passageway of her flat, a mirror leans against the wall, shoes lie discarded where they were taken off. Letters and a magazine are strewn casually on the floor. She uses her foot to push the door closed. Her legs are longer than I remember.

Ivan has rung; his words are short and clipped. "I'm going to be late, an emergency."

"How late?"

"I don't know. . . ." His voice softens.

I think he is going to say something about this morning or my message. He doesn't. If he were telepathic, he would hear me saying, "*You never had sex with her, did you?*" It would have had a sympathetic tone but underneath it he would detect the sarcasm.

I sit in the living room and watch the furniture as it turns gray and disappears.

At ten o'clock I turn the television on. It is Ivan's television. A monster. Twenty-eight inches of color. Apart from the bag of his clothes, this is what he brought with him when he moved in. Before he moved in, he used to spend his evenings in his bed-sit, lying on his bed, holding the aerial to get a picture on his television. Each channel required a slightly altered position. This is what he told me. I arranged an outdoor aerial immediately. This simple thing made him extremely happy. Before, when there was no television, I listened to the news on the radio. On the television I watch the news with the sound turned down. A small child's face smiling, then pictures of empty fields under a harsh sun. A line of police beating at the ground with sticks. (It is the second day of this search.) Next, pictures of soldiers and fighting. Then a crowd burning effigies somewhere where all the buildings are painted white and there are avenues with traffic islands full of trees. A line of refugees, sodden with rain, bags heavy on their backs. The newscaster smiles and there are pictures of cricket. Then the weather. Southeast England has clouds with forked lines emerging from them; I go into the kitchen and remove the saucepans from the cupboard under the sink. George watches; he already knows a storm is coming. He crawls in, lies down. I leave the door slightly ajar and think how I am always tempted to join him.

In bed I think of Ivan's face. What I would say if he went

missing. If he didn't come home. What I would do. Two nights with emergencies is rare. I could ring him, but he might think I was needy. This is not an impression I have ever liked to give. I myself do not like neediness. In either the male or the female version.

Sometimes I think he has not given up his bed-sit in Finsbury Park. That this is where he goes when he says there is an emergency. He waited six months after he moved in with me before he gave his notice. He said there was always a chance we might not work out. I had to concede.

The consoling thought: the television is here now. The other way of looking at it. He could have bought a new one.

I get up, phone the old number. The man who answers sounds drunk. He sounded drunk the last time I rang, a month ago.

"Is Ivan there?"

"Who?"

I flick through my address book. I could ring some of the numbers I come across. But I have no desire to talk to any of the people listed. They always ask questions that refer in some way to the past. Especially those I used to work with in the library. By the name of each person is the date I last spoke to him or her marked neatly in red pen. There is not one date that is less than a year ago.

I get to *W.* Yes, there is. I remember the smiling face of Tina Willis. The date of ringing her is less than six months ago. I will update her on George.

I don't recognize the voice that answers the phone.

"Is Tina Willis there?"

"She moved out in February."

I use a red pen to score out the name from the address book.

The table on Ivan's side of the bed seems to stare at me. I open the drawer, lift out the cigar box, take it to the bathroom. I make sure to lock the door in case Ivan comes home. I unfold all the bits of tissue paper and lay the hair, the photograph and the drawing on top of the chair.

The hair is soft and has the faintest smell of smoke. The photograph offers no more information. Except the fact that as well as kissing they are both smiling. I hold the drawing of the swans progressing to hearts up to the light. There is a tiny grease stain on the left-hand corner. I look again at his old passport. Before in his picture all I saw was his youth. Now I see a look of longing and sadness in his eyes. I look at the stamps to Canada. I put my finger in my mouth to wet it, rub at one of them. It does not smear. Not that this tells me anything. I repack everything as I found it. As I do, I imagine burning them one by one in the kitchen sink. Catching sight of myself in the mirror, I grow aware of the ridiculous aspect of the situation: I am approaching forty, and the girl I am worried about still exists in Ivan's mind at the age of sixteen.

Ivan slides into bed beside me at midnight.

"Did you eat any supper?" I ask.

"Chinese," he says.

"I ate oranges—both of them."

I think he smiles but I cannot tell in the dark.

I can just make out his hands folded on his chest.

Usually he draws me close to him. Tonight there is a sense we are both outlined in black. Separate. As I move closer to him he turns his back to me. I am not sure if he is sulking or angry. The first flash of lightning streams across the ceiling and I wait for the noise to follow. I count the seconds, work out the miles. It rumbles toward us as I reach ten.

matches
candle
flint
magnifying glass
needles and thread
fishhooks and line
compass
beta light
snare wire
flexible saw
medical kit:
    analgesic
    intestinal sedative
    antibiotic
    antihistamine
    water-sterilizing tablets
    antimalaria tablets
    potassium permanganate
    surgical blades x 2
    butterfly sutures
    plasters
    condom (for water-bag)

mess tin
solid fuel tablets in stove container
pencil-like torch
flares, green and red miniflares
tea powder & sachets of milk and sugar
electrolite powderheat-insulated bag (7 ft × 2 ft)
   200 cm × 60 cm
food:
   2 Kendal mint cake/chocolate
   5 tins sardines in tomato
   1 pkt of Ryvita
windup radio
GPS watch
clear plastic bags
mobile phone

Ivan sleeps. I sit cross-legged in the passageway, lay the contents of my rucksack out in a circle around me: the contents dictated by *The SAS Survival Handbook* that is also carefully packed.

Additional items:

a bottle of lavender oil and a bottle of tea tree oil
a bottle of spirulina tablets and a jar of 90 1,000-mg
   vitamin C capsules
Tiger Balm (white, extra strength)
a warm red jumper
a green waterproof jacket
one pair thick black socks

a bottle of still mineral water
a roll of white toilet paper
sanitary provisions for two months
a blue comb and five blue elastic hair bands
a bar of all-purpose soap
a week's supply of underwear, all cotton, all black
a head scarf, a sunhat, a pair of polarized sunglasses
a box of dried cat food
a Swiss Army knife
£100 in £20 notes rolled and held together with a rubber
    band with a Post-it stuck to it reminding me to displace
    it around my body: sock, shoe, bra, trouser pocket, hat

If I ever have to go out, I am ready.

Outside the front door, I can hear a voice. Mrs. Heksa talking to someone just behind her front door. I can't hear the words; the tone sounds as if she is consoling a child. A roll of thunder drowns her words. It is quiet again.

I counted the money before I put it back in the rucksack. There is more than there should be. And in fifty-pound notes, not twenties. A thousand pounds, the notes clean and crisp. There is also money in the back pocket that runs the width and length of the bag. It was not there when I checked last week; neat wads of fifty-pound notes, each held tight by a light green paper band. Total amount fifty-thousand pounds.

THURSDAY

I can see it from the balcony. A black car parked at the corner of the street. Inside it is Skye but she shouldn't look like Skye. As instructed, she shouldn't be wearing anything floral. As instructed, she should be wearing black, with a scarf tied around her head to hide her hair and dark glasses to cover her face. She is waiting for my signal. She will have carefully arranged the hands-free wire from her mobile phone so it doesn't show.

"Is it time?" she says when she picks up my call, and she takes a drag on her cigarette.

"It is time," I tell her.

I hear her turn the key, the sound of the engine, her feet arranging themselves against the pedals, the creak of her seat as she leans to look in the sideview mirror.

"I see him," she says.

"I see him too," I say.

Ivan opens the door of his van, gets in, closes the door, rolls down his window and pulls out and away. I hear the bangles on Skye's wrist clink together as she changes gear. The echo of Ivan's car as it passes hers. She pulls out and follows.

"All right?" I ask her.

"All right," she says.

The indicator sounds as she turns left and out of my view. She turns on the radio before she hangs up.

I made the arrangements before Ivan woke: one phone call to Skye, one phone call to our mother to arrange to take Skye's kids, one phone call to a car-hire company. At breakfast Ivan and I ate our oranges as we used to do, in sync, the little piles of peel building up to the right-hand sides of the plates. I was all smiles. I asked no questions. We both laughed as George emerged sleepily from the cupboard.

"You look tired," Ivan had said.

"I know," I said back.

"Are you ill, Miss Moneypenny?" he asked as he stroked my hair.

"No, just tired," I had said.

I have made two phone calls. I have placed two orders. The first courier arrives at 10:20 and the second at 10:24. The first package is cylindrical, the size of a hatbox. The second the size of a matchbox. It is taped to another small box with the words "cleaning fluid" written on the side.

Ash blond hair. Green eyes. I walk across the bedroom and back. My step is lighter. My shoulders more relaxed. I seem thinner than I usually do. All traces of makeup have been removed. The palest powder I can find has been applied. I look like the label that describes it: translucent. Like someone who has spent too long under moonlight. The shadows under my eyes seem somehow fitting. In the mirror in the bedroom, in the mirror in the bathroom, in the mirror in the treatment room, in the mirror in the passageway, in all of them me as Sophia. Ash blond hair and green eyes. The wig is shoulder length, middle part, no fringe. The contact lenses nonprescription. The whites of my eyes are not as red as they were when I first put the lenses in.

"Page 73–4J: Montgomery Road." I repeat the coordinates as I find the page in the A–Z. I put my finger on the road.

"Did you see who answered the door?" I ask.

"Female . . . fiftyish," Skye says.

"Attractive?" I ask.

"Well groomed," is her answer.

"Did you take a photograph?"

"Yes."

"How long has he been there?"

"Half an hour."

"Anything else?"

"He went to a shop and bought some things—piping, it looked like."

"An ironmonger's?"

"Yeah—an ironmonger's, copper piping, long lengths of it."

"Talk to you later."

"Laters," she says.

"You look tired," Ivan had said.

"I know," I said back.

"Are you ill, Miss Moneypenny?" he asked as he stroked my hair.

"No, just tired," I had said.

I have done the breathing exercises. In through the nose as far as you can, hold and out in six small short bursts through the mouth. I have inhaled lavender in large quantity. I have pinched my ears and rubbed my eyebrows. I have tried every remedy for tiredness I know. They have not worked. I drink coffee. Extra strong and extra sweet. The coffee Skye brings for her visits. Ethiopian. Full strength. The first coffee I have drunk in a long time. Bits of blond hair keep catching on my lips. Already I've acquired the habit of tucking it behind my ears. I imagine she would resist such a habit. Letting it always fall to frame her face, the green eyes peeping seductively from behind its drape. I make myself aware. Stop my hand as it reaches to do it again, run my fingers through the hair instead. My heart races as my liver releases another dose of glucose into the blood. I listen again for the hiss. Last night in the hallway the gas was strong and I could hear a soft hissing sound, but this morning it had gone although the smell is still there. George sleeps on my lap. He is indifferent to my new blond hair, my new green eyes. I drink more coffee. I wait for Skye to ring. I clock-watch. I have canceled all my clients with the excuse of a summer cold and an injured hand; their concern was touching. I have cleaned the tape mark from the window. Ivan had done the shopping. Including the lighter fuel. Today he needs to do no shopping. We will have the meal planned for last night tonight. If he does not need to do the shopping he should be back at six. Not seven.

Skye says, "Page 90—C2: Melville Road. Nothing unusual. I'm bored."

I find the page in the *A–Z* and put my finger on the road.

"Did you hear me?—I'm bored, and it's very hot."

I say, "Buy a newspaper. Smoke another cigarette. Have a cold drink."

And Skye hangs up.

I gaze again at Sophia in the mirror. I have been doing that a lot. The last few times I have smiled as I did it. An involuntary reaction.

I will wait in the kitchen for Ivan when he comes home. He will see me and stop in his tracks, and a smile will pass across his face as he again makes his way toward me. Standing next to me, he will lean toward me and tip my chin up with his fingers so he can look into my green eyes, and as he does so, he will lean closer and kiss me. His eyes will have the steeliness of understanding and the grateful welling of tears. After the kiss, tender. Gentle. Almost without passion but full of adoration (for me. For what I have done for him—not for her—not for Sophia), he will stoop down to slide an arm under the crook of my bent knees and slide the other arm across my shoulder blades, the tips of his fingers coming to rest at the side of my breast. The muscles in his arms will tighten against my body as he lifts me. He'll have to kick the chair out from under the table as he does this. With ease he'll carry me down the passageway to the bedroom and carefully lay me on the bed.

"Hello," she calls through the door as she hears me approach.

"Yes."

Through the peephole I can see she is still wearing her pajamas. Tartan. Burberry. Her hair is wrapped in a white towel.

"I was putting my rubbish outside to take it down, and the door slammed behind me. I'm locked out."

She has raised her eyes to the ceiling as if cursing herself and hoping I will help. "Can I climb over your balcony?"

Sophia would not continue this conversation through the door. Sophia would open it and greet the stranger cordially.

I unlock the door.

She puts her hand out to shake mine. Her hands are frail as little birds, but her hold is firm.

"Catrina," she says.

"Sophia," I say. There is no hesitation. There is no difficulty in saying the name. It does not stick in my throat.

"Pleased to meet you," she says. She squeezes my hand a little tighter before releasing it. Her eyes do not linger on any part of my face for too long as if anything is not quite right. I feel the thrill of telling a lie. A slight blush. A hint of sweat at the hairline. The one underneath the wig.

I lead her down the passageway and into the kitchen and out onto the balcony.

"Thank you," she says as she begins to maneuver across, her long legs striding over nimble and fast. She talks as she moves. "I've got two letters, I think they're yours—they were put in my post box by mistake . . . yesterday."

When she gets to her balcony she turns back to me. "I was going to drop them in—or do you want to come over?"

She waits for my answer.

"Can you drop them over?" I say as I wonder if it was before or after she came back from the park and why she didn't drop them over last night.

She looks curiously at me. "Are you sure you don't want a coffee?"

Sophia would be easygoing. Sophia would say, "Yeah." Sophia would probably go across the balcony.

"Expecting a call," I say.

"Hold on," she says.

She is in and out of her flat and leans over the railing, letters in hand. "Sorry, I opened one of them before checking."

I want to ask her where she is from. Sometimes her accent is French. Sometimes it's American.

"Ivan—is that your man?" she asks. She is looking at the bracelet as she gives me the letters.

I give her a smile that means yes.

"I've always loved that name. Mysterious sounding. Goes so well with Sophia."

I notice her eyes are more green than blue. They seem to change with the light.

"I'll be in all day if you change your mind," she says as she moves back inside.

77

Ivan is in West London. He starts farthest out and zigzags in toward home. He has good strategy. Each visit averages an hour and a half. He bought a sandwich for lunch and ate it as he walked along the pavement.

At three-thirty in Notting Hill Gate she went into a news-agent's to get more cigarettes and while she was in there, Ivan came in to get some chocolate. That is what Skye tells me.

"What you doing in this neck of the woods?" he had said.

"Job interview," she said.

In the street, as they were about to part, he had asked her if I had mentioned anything to her about money, because he knows I talk to Skye about everything.

"What money?" she asks me.

"I'll tell you later," I say.

"Will you?"

"Yes."

"He doesn't suspect anything. He didn't see the car," she says.

"So keep following him."

"I have," she says. "Page 75–H1: Aubrey Walk."

"What else did you talk about?"

"His pictures. The girls—not much, he was in a rush."

Skye rang again twenty minutes later.

He went into a hotel near Knightsbridge station. He came out again almost immediately. He came out talking to a man. The man slapped Ivan on the back and then they were laughing.

"I've got a picture," said Skye.

"Young man or old man?"

"Looked about the same age as Ivan." Skye is being polite. "Dark hair," she added.

"Where is he now?"

"They went into the tube station."

"And . . . ?"

I told her to wait near his van. To wait and see if and when he came back. To call me and tell me and then to go home.

He came back at 5:36. He was carrying a bag he didn't have before.

"What do you want me to do?" asks Skye.

"Go home—he'll be on his way back. I'll call you later."

I waited for Ivan in the kitchen. He stopped in his tracks when he saw me. For what seemed like a long time, he took stock. No smile crossed his face as he moved toward me. He circled slowly around me rattling his keys. And then he put the keys down on the table and circled once more. I looked at my hands resting on the table. I used the hair to shield my eyes from him. He came around to the back of me. I could feel the slight weight of his hip against my shoulder. He

79

made a noise with his fingernails, working his thumbnail across the other nails, flicking them. It is what he does when he is unsure of what to say. His hands shook as he stroked my hair. Not my hair. The "ash blond" hair. Her hair. He stroked it with both hands at the same time, one on either side of my head, from the crown down to the ears to the shoulders. Hardly touching it at all. It was then his breathing changed. Quickened and staggered as if he were holding back tears. He came around to the front of me; there were no tears. He placed one hand on the side of each of my shoulders and pulled me up to standing and tilted my head up. His touch was gentle. I kept my face very still. Kept my eyes from meeting his. Played dead. The game I learned as a child. But he turned my head so my eyes met his. And because he looked at her and not at me and because I did not want to be invisible, I smiled. I knew as I did it, it was the wrong thing. I knew underneath it all his gentleness could move to something else. The wig did not come off when he hit me. I had pinned it tight. I had expected it could go this way. It was part of the bargain.

He carried me to the bedroom. It was awkward; he stumbled with my weight and I scraped my elbow against the wall of the passageway. But it didn't matter; he didn't register these things. He had shifted somewhere else. He was no longer there.

Things didn't go as I had expected. He couldn't do it. He laid me down on the bed. We kissed. We undressed each other. But when it came to the act, he couldn't do it. He seemed more upset than angry. He dressed with his back to me and left the room. Didn't say a word.

He is in the kitchen. I heard the chair as he pulled it out to sit down. I imagine he is looking at the letter Catrina Heksa brought over, the one she opened by mistake.

I left it on the table. He had put his keys down on it. I can hear the slight clink of the keys as he lifts them.

I think maybe I planned it badly doing what I did before I had cooked supper. I should have done it later. After supper. Now there will be no supper. I do not feel like eating; neither will Ivan. Already I can hear him being sick in the bathroom. Anxiety does that to him. Makes him sick. Maybe it's not just me and what I did (and what he couldn't do); I know it's not. It's also because he knows I have seen what is in the letter.

I can hear him moving up the passageway toward me. I don't want to discuss it now. I'm tired; all I want to do is sleep. I lie down, close my eyes. I can sense him watching me from the doorway. He has the letter in his hands; I hear him unfold it and fold it again. I still don't open my eyes. He turns and goes, moves down the passageway to the living room, puts the television on. I take out the green eyes but leave on the wig.

Tonight he will sleep on the sofa; I know he will. It is a necessary gesture. Things did not go the way I had expected, but I notice the smell of gas is not as strong as it was earlier.

In the middle of the night, I wake; he is sitting on the edge of the bed staring at me.

"What is it?"

"Nothing."

He gets up and leaves the room, takes a blanket and a pillow.

I fall asleep again thinking about the letter, a savings statement, zeros extending to hundreds of thousands. Ivan is a very rich man. For a man who's supposed to be a gas fitter. For a man who deals with problems relating to gas.

"I want to tell you about the money," Ivan says, indicating the letter lying on the table with a nod of his head. His voice is calm. Matter-of-fact. Very formal. Like breakfast has been. Overpolite. Extra normal. Bits of orange peel exactly placed. Water sipped noiselessly. I have asked him no questions. He pushes at a bit of orange peel with his finger. Folds his arms and leans back on his chair. (He folds his arms when he is nervous. And to tell me he is serious.)

"It's not my money, I'm just looking after it."

His voice lowering to a concerned whisper: "He's a gambler—he's a good gambler, but he doesn't know when to stop. . . . I look after the winnings for him—so he can't get at it. . . . Do you believe me?"

I break a piece of orange peel into smaller pieces. Soon I will tell him I don't care about the money. Soon but not yet.

He leans over and removes a strand of the blond hair that

has caught on my mouth. He kisses my face where he hit me. It is the second time he has done this.

The first time there was an apology. This time he says, "You shouldn't have smiled like that—you made me feel like a cunt."

"I didn't mean to," I tell him. I lean my head into the hand he has cupped over my cheek.

Breakfast has been strange. Breakfast has been awkward. And romantic. Underneath the table my shoes are blue.

"Did you think I was going to use it to go to Canada?" The Scottish accent thick.

He has his hand over mine, fingering the bracelet; he slides a finger underneath where the name is, slides it against my skin. Back and forth he moves his finger as he smiles at me. "If I wanted to go, I could have gone already."

He lifts his hand to smooth my hair. "It really suits you being blond." His voice pure sex.

I have seen film of opposite tides meeting at sea. Each tide tries to get through to the other side. As they do, they bind with each other. Lift to create a swell. This is what it feels like this morning, what is happening between him and me. Sometimes that and sometimes something very fragile. If it had a sound, it would be the purposeful and delicate scuttle of a beetle across a wooden floor. This is what I think.

I follow him into the passageway and watch him as he puts on his jacket. Today he seems taller. Today I feel a little scared of Ivan. I am thinking, "You should never start what you can't finish." It is something my father used to tell me.

He unlocks the door, turns. "See you later, sweetheart."

I watch him descend the stairs, move back inside in time to watch him get into his van. He puts his hand out of the window to wave. He is smiling as he drives away.

I did not do a shopping list. It seemed inappropriate. Too domestic. Unromantic.

I watch him at the end of the street. The indicator is blinking but he has not turned left. I wave, turn, move inside. He has told me that as he drives away in the morning he likes to watch me in his sideview mirror moving from the balcony to inside the flat. He says he finds it comforting knowing I will be there all day. That he can always place me in his thoughts.

"Okra. Garlic. Tomatoes. Basmati rice. Coriander." Skye repeats the list after me.

"Come at one o'clock, let yourself in."

"Okay."

"Skye."

"What?"

"Don't be surprised when you see me: I'm wearing a wig."

I hear her take a drag of her cigarette, the clink of her bangles. "A blond wig?"

"Yes."

"Are you sure you know what you're doing?"

"Yes."

I am talking to the dial tone. I phone her again. "What happened?"

"I dropped the phone."

"Skye."

"What?"

"I also have a bruise on my face; I opened the medical cabinet too quickly."

(I do not want her to ask questions. I do not want her to have more reasons not to like Ivan.)

"Don't forget the photographs," I tell her, and I put down the phone.

I have changed the middle part to a side part to hide the mark on my face. I have also used flesh-colored concealer. I collect George from the bedroom, where he is sleeping. Put him in the kitchen. Close all the doors as I walk down the passageway, go into the treatment room, put on my white coat. Check my appointments.

10:00 Mrs. Barver-Reiss
11:30 Mrs. Toume
2:00 Mrs. Klein
4:00 Mrs. O'Connor

Mrs Barver-Reiss compliments me on my new hair. She says, "It is very becoming," when I open the door. Perhaps I smile too generously.

As I lead her into the treatment room, she says, "You seem much happier today." It is an intrusive comment to make. Her well-being is my business. My well-being is not her business. Her comment also suggests my appearance is normally the opposite. I don't know how to respond to her observation. I don't know what to say. I hand her the questionnaire without looking at her and leave her to change. I sit and wait for her in the passageway. She probably thinks with my new hair I will be more friendly. *"You seem happier today."* It is an intrusive comment to make. But it is true. There is something lighter about my disposition; I can feel it. I think. It has been there since Ivan said, "It really suits you being blond." His voice pure sex.

I wait for the creak of the table as she gets on it. Give her a moment. Enter. Check her questionnaire. "Aging, Feelings of"; "Boredom"; "Critical of Others."

The scent of the rosewood is floral with spicy undertones.

Catrina Heksa is on the landing as I open the door to see Mrs. Barver-Reiss out. A hand poised ready to knock. Her eyes seem greener. Her hair remains hidden under a pale lilac scarf. Her white dress is of the sun variety, thin straps.

"Hi, Sophia," she says. Her voice seems to have more of a drawl today.

She moves aside to let Mrs. Barver-Reiss pass, waiting until Mrs. Barver-Reiss has started to descend the stairs before she hands me the two letters I can see she is carrying.

"The postman must think Ivan lives with me." She smiles as she passes the letters to me.

I apologize as I take the letters, but her comment makes me nervous. Unthinking, my other hand is at my hair, tucking it behind my ear. The smile drops from her mouth.

"Did something happen to your face?"

"Nothing serious."

"Looks nasty."

"It looks worse than it is." I untuck the hair, use the letters to cover my cheek.

I take a step back, begin to close the door. "I'm expecting a client. I'd better go."

She continues to hover at the threshold. She eyes my white coat. "Are you an osteopath?"

"An aroma—"

"—therapist." She finishes off the word, nods her head as if pleased with herself. "I'm a researcher. . . ."

She notices how my gaze dips to her basket, containing the blanket that is balanced in the crook of her elbow. "I'm on leave—to move in. . . . I'm on my way to the park."

I say nothing.

She still does not go. She smiles at me again. "I prefer you blond. I meant to tell you that yesterday."

I resist the need to touch my hair. I look at my feet.

I look at her feet: silver strapped sandals. Toenails painted to match.

I lift my head and smile benevolently. "I really must go."

She puts her hand on the door as I begin to close it. "Does Ivan have one green eye and one blue eye?"

"Yes."

"Thought it was him. . . . Some other time—for coffee then."

She smiles again and I close the door.

I watch her from the balcony as she walks lazily down the path. She senses me watching, turns, looks and waves. My hand goes up and waves back. It was involuntary. Yesterday was the first day I had ever seen her. I thought it was also the first time she had seen me. I wonder why she said nothing about the color of my eyes. I feel more cheated than stupid.

The letters are credit-card applications. One addressed to Mr. Ivan Turner. One addressed to Mr. Steven Turner. This does not alarm me. Ivan has told me it is a common mistake. I tear the letters up, put them in the bin. Ivan and I do not agree with credit. We have discussed it. We both think one should live within one's means. I reapply the flesh-colored concealer. Add powder.

Zeros extending to hundreds of thousands. I have been thinking about the savings statement as I waited for Mrs. Toume. What Ivan's means really are. If he is lying about the gambler. If he lied about going to Canada, he could be lying about the gambler.

I imagine the sort of light breeze that amount of money would make if you could hold it in your hand and fan it with a thumb.

The breeze is cool. The breeze is cold.

I have rung Ivan.

The question I asked him: "Are you going to Canada? Is that what the money is really for?"

The answer he gave me: "Miss Moneypenny. You should know better than that. What do I need to go to Canada for—I've got you!" The Scottish accent thick.

It is true. I am inside. Locked up. Available.

. . .

Mrs. Toume, my new client, announces herself on the intercom. I smooth down my white coat, open the door and wait for her to come up the stairs. When she sees me she looks at me suspiciously.

"Ms. Lewis?"

"Yes?"

"Are you sure?"

"Excuse me?"

"Sorry—it was just . . . I was told you were a redhead."

"I am Ms. Lewis. It is a change of hair color, nothing more," I reassure her. As I am speaking I can feel a slight pressure against my skin, from the inside pushing out. And heat. I am blushing; my body knows I am lying.

"I apologize: I didn't mean to embarrass you," she says as I show her in.

I say nothing, hand her a questionnaire and leave her to change.

On her questionnaire she had ticked "Mental Rigidity." Twice during our session she complained I was using too much pressure.

I liked her a little better as she paid me: she counted out the tens into my hand.

Skye has arrived. As well as my shopping she has been clothes shopping. Braided handles adorn her shoulders.

Today the nails of Skye's feet and hands are painted pink to match the flowers on her shirt. It is a new shirt. Her shoes are also new. These days she always seems to have new clothes. Even though she always claims she's broke.

She puts the bags down on the kitchen floor. I stand to greet her.

She stares at me. Her thoughts making the connection—I can see it in her eyes—between the wearing of the wig and the bruise on my face. She stretches out her fingers and holds them lightly on the bruise, moves them to my chin to turn my head to the light and inspects the swelling.

She asks, looking at my head, "Did Ivan like it?"

"I think so."

I am not sure if I want to tell her about his impotence. Not yet.

She sits down at the kitchen table, surveys me. "Did you put some ice on the bruise?"

"Ice and arnica," I tell her. I have done neither: I want the mark to linger a while.

"Do you need to be somewhere?" I ask her.

The way she flicks the foot of her crossed leg up and down as if she is restless and impatient to be off.

"Shortly," she says as she takes the envelope of photographs from her bag.

I lay them down side by side on the kitchen table. She's taken two or three in each place; some of them are out of focus.

There is:

Ivan against the backdrop of a small semidetached with a
    red door
Ivan against a white stucco town house
Ivan against a privet hedge

Ivan against a front garden filled with nettles and an old
  mattress
Ivan coming down a gravel path. He looks as if he is
  whistling
Ivan eating his sandwich as he walks in the street

Two pictures show a glimpse of the person he was visiting;
a hand curled around a door as it's being opened or being
held open; Ivan is wiping his feet; a woman's profile as she
is turning to show Ivan in. ("The well-groomed fifty-year-
old," Skye says, pointing.)

The last picture: Ivan and the man outside the hotel. The
man is handsome. His face wide as Ivan's is narrow. His hair
dark and curly. His mouth full like Ivan's. Good teeth. His
suit is expensive—well cut. The jacket sits well on his broad
shoulders. He is a man who excites the visual cortex. He is
the reason Skye is suddenly smiling.

I give her the rundown; the fifty-thousand pounds in cash,
the savings statement that runs into hundreds of thousands;
the "gambler." I point to the man in the picture.

I tell her, "I want you to go to the hotel again. I need to
know if Ivan is there again today."

She says, "All that money. All these secrets."

She tilts her head, shifts her weight farther back in the
chair. She stares at me. Bruise to hair and back. "I want you
to tell me what happened to your face," she says.

She waits. I know it is the deal: she will go to the hotel
only if I tell her.

I explain what happened last night. Ivan's inability to perform. I inform her of the conversation with Ivan's mother. I tell her how he lied about "Canada."

"God, Stella—how terrible . . . how awful for you," she says, sweet as honey, taking my hand. She stares at my hair. At the wig.

I shrug my shoulders. "I like the change. Ivan liked the change."

She raises her eyebrows. Her foot starts to flick up and down again as it did before. She looks at her watch.

"Do you have to go?"

"Yes, I have to go now."

"Laters," she says as I see her out.

I watch her leave from the balcony. Her diamanté sandals flash in the sunlight as she walks to her car. Today, with her elegant outfit, she should have parted with something more European. Au revoir. Ciao. Auf Wiedersehen. She gets into the car; I can see her checking herself in the rearview mirror. She reapplies her lipstick, rolls down the window, puts on her sunglasses, turns on the radio. Pop music blares out too loudly. I watch her drive to the end of the street and turn left. I wonder why Ivan did not mention his meeting with her yesterday.

Under the kitchen table is a loose floorboard; this is where I hide the photographs.

"Hi, sweetheart," he says as he picks up the phone.

Their meeting: Skye had told me she was in the newsagent's and he came in and he asked what she was doing in that "neck of the woods." Ivan told me he was in a newsagent's and suddenly someone stroked the back of his neck. He had turned; he didn't recognize her at first; she had on dark glasses and a scarf.

Her flicking foot. Her restlessness. She was expecting questions.

"Did you tell Skye about last night?" he had asked me.

"Would it be a problem if I had?"

"I don't think it would be a good idea."

Under a film of plastic, on the underside of the telephone, the list of people whose numbers are assigned to memory are printed out neatly. Number one is Ivan. Number two is Skye's mobile. I press number two. It rings once. I put the phone down: If I confront her now, if I question her, she may not go to the hotel for me. If I ask her if she lied, she may also think I am suggesting something else. We could end up being estranged again.

I reapply the flesh-colored concealer to cover the bruise and comb my hair. I put in the green lenses. I close my eyes, wait for the irritation to fade. She does not like him; she has said so on numerous occasions. It disturbs me, that he said she touched his neck to greet him. People do not touch people they do not like. They avoid contact.

Her hand on his forearm.

Her hand on his upper arm.

Her hand on his back.

The careful and considered removal of cat hair from the leg of his trousers.

It is a backdated noticing. A flick-book catalog.

Skye uses every opportunity to touch Ivan.

S.L:

Sophia Lawrence.

Stella Lewis.

Skye Lewis.

To a glass of water I add five drops of Bach Flower Remedy White Chestnut for "constant worrying thoughts and/or mental arguments." I note I need to order another bottle.

Mrs. Klein arrives promptly at two o'clock. She remarks immediately how the blond hair lifts my skin tones and brings out the color of my eyes. She has not noticed that my eye color has changed from blue to green. I am gracious. I say, "Thank you," and show her into the treatment room. I sense she wants to touch me. Or kiss me on the cheek. I hand her the questionnaire and leave her to change.

During our session I see her notice the bruise on my face. She looks away. Focuses on the ceiling. I am grateful that she does not ask questions.

"Did you hear about Mrs. Jones?" she asks after a moment.

"I'd rather not discuss other clients."

"Well . . . anyway, the treatment you gave her seemed to work."

She closes her eyes. She says nothing more on the subject. She lingers at the front door as I see her out and smiles at me.

"See you next week, Mrs. Klein."

"Good-bye, Ms. Lewis."

I watch her take the stairs, and then I close the door.

George is locked in Catrina Heksa's flat. I can hear him scratching against the glass of her balcony doors.

The scratching stops. Silence. A long-drawn-out meow, and he begins to scratch again, more frantic and determined.

"It's okay, George, I'm coming."

I keep my voice calm. If he senses I am panicking, so will he. I undo the buttons on my white coat, remove it and fold it and place it carefully over the chair on the balcony. I do it slowly to defy my quickened heartbeat and my throat that is constricting with a held-back sob. I walk to the railing I must climb, look down; it is thirty feet to the path below. If I fall I will land where the others landed. Half on one of the flower beds, half on the path. Limbs arranged like a swastika. George senses what I am about to do, meows pitifully. The scratching builds to a frenzy. I take a deep breath in through the nose and then out through the mouth, turn inward to face the bricks, fixing my focus on the mortar as my hands clutch the metal. I count to ten, lever myself over the railing, over the small gap, less than four inches, onto her balcony. Swing my other leg over. The scratching stops.

The door is locked. I was hoping it had only been pulled to. I only ever pull mine to. George presses his body against the glass, sits and stares at me, offers me another long-drawn-out meow. I kneel down in front of him.

"Why are you in there?"

He yawns, resumes his scratching and meowing as I stand and move away, climb back over the railing.

"Hi, it's Ms. Lewis."

"Hello, Stella." The caretaker of the flats continues to ignore my request for a more formal exchange.

He informs me he has already given Catrina Heksa the spare key as she had lost her own and needed to get another cut.

He says I should wait. She'll be home soon.

"She'll be out all day. . . . She's gone to the park. . . ." I tell him.

When he hears the sob break in my voice, he adds suggestively that all the keys for the balcony doors are the same.

"A safety precaution."

George watches as I unlock the door. Impatient. Meowing. I open the door. He shoots by me and out. I watch as he charges over the gap and goes into my kitchen. I know he is heading for the bathroom, for his litter tray. I have trained him well. I should follow him home. I look across the threshold into the room. I step into it.

It smells of fresh paint and sleep.

To my right a double futon. White sheets. Unmade. On the floor a large black suitcase, open, clothes lazily thrown in. On the back of the room door, pale clothing slung without care on hangers. Draped over the handle, the scarf she was wearing yesterday. It is how I imagine Sophia would live. This casualness. There are dust balls on the bare floorboards that look as if they've been there so long they should have names.

I walk across the room and lift the scarf from the door handle, sniff it. It smells of shampoo. This suggests she does have hair. I glance around the room searching for a hairbrush, cannot see one. It must be in the bathroom, I think. I open the door and go into the passageway.

In the passageway the full-length mirror rests against the wall. Next to it the shoes left as they have been kicked off. Two pairs of identical sandals. Simple and modest, with a small heel. One in black. One in white. The ones she was wearing when I opened my door to her were the same in silver. There is also a pair of man's sandals and a pair of man's trainers. He has big feet. Size eleven. Like Ivan. I slip off my blue shoes. Slip on her white sandals, note the way they set off my new blond hair. I view them from all angles. Skye would approve.

By the shoes a letter. I crouch down to read it. A confirmation of delivery dates from a furniture shop. One chest of drawers. Beech. One wardrobe. Beech. One double bed. Beech. Catrina Heksa is casual but aims for harmony. Maybe she senses it is needed; I wonder if the caretaker has told her the two previous occupiers both attempted suicide by jumping from the balcony. I wonder if I should tell her. I wonder if she will keep her clothes neatly in the wardrobe.

I leave the shoes on as I hunt for the hairbrush.

The living room is bare except for a beanbag, a chair, a television and a vacuum cleaner. Lifestyle and decorating magazines lie open at various pages on the floor. Two pages have been torn out and are stuck to the wall. A picture of the three-piece bedroom set, the one that she has ordered in beech. A picture of a sofa. A sofa without soft furnishing. Modular. Cinema seats in style. She tends to minimalist, I think. But I note the rich pink-and-gold sari material being used as a curtain. A sensual minimalist.

The hairbrush is lying on the corner of the bath. A single gray hair lies among its bristles. I look in the bin under the sink. A lone ball of matted hair, no doubt cleaned from the brush, lies at its new white plastic bottom. I take the hair out, carry it into the passageway to hold it under the skylight. It is mostly gray. But there is also black and there is also silver blond. I place it back in the bin. I open and smell the shampoo to confirm it is the same as that on the scarf. It is. I continue down the passageway.

The room that in my flat is my treatment room is filled with cardboard boxes of varying sizes waiting to be unpacked. I would open them to investigate but they are sealed shut with parcel tape; she has not bothered to label the outsides of the boxes. She will regret this.

Her kitchen is where my bedroom is, by the front door. Nothing remarkable. Not yet. I noticed the kitchen she had marked out in one of the magazines. She has big plans. She must also have money. There is a garden table and two matching chairs. Two newspapers lie on the table: a tabloid and a broadsheet. Both appear unread. In the drying-up rack, two cups, two plates, two sets of cutlery. One saucepan on the stove. I open the cupboard above the work surface. A pot of strawberry jam. Half a dozen eggs. A packet of salt. A small clear plastic tub containing what resembles dried herbs. The label COSMIC C . . . printed in red on the side. As I lean and twist the tub to read the other word I hear the distinctive sound of a key being inserted into a lock. I look at the other word. I think, "I could stay." I could confront her now. I look at my feet. Her shoes. I decide I'd rather not, calculating there is still time to get out. There are three locks to the door.

I close the cupboard door. I take her shoes off, run on tiptoe down the passageway, place her shoes by the mirror, snatch up my own shoes, can hear the key in the second lock. I am through her balcony door before I hear the third lock. But haven't yet closed it. I hear her say, "Fuck." I know what has happened: the through draft has slammed the front door against her as she opened it.

I close her balcony door and quickly lock it. Glance again into her room. If I come again I will make the bed and fold the clothes in the suitcase.

I climb back over the railings.

I have given George three large pinches of catnip. He did not seem that interested. It is not as fresh or as "cosmic" as the one in Catrina Heksa's kitchen cupboard.

I have sat him on my lap and rubbed his ears; it is a well-known fact that the more affectionate you are to cats, the more affectionate they are back.

I think maybe I should adopt the same approach to Ivan. I think about what people say—it is not unfaithfulness that is the issue, it is the reason why it happens in the first place.

I have not been so attentive to George of late.

It takes two to tango. There is always temptation.

I watch him as he sleeps on the kitchen chair. He opens one eye, closes it again, sighs; he is indifferent to my anxiety.

I think again about Catrina Heksa's white sandals. How good they looked on my feet. As I walk down the passageway to the bathroom, I hear Catrina Heksa's door closing.

I walk back to the kitchen and onto the balcony and wait for her to appear on the path. She takes her time; she should be out by now. I imagine she is checking her post box. Finally there is the sound of heels on the stone stairs to the path. She swings her basket as she makes her way, her walk slow and unconcerned. I keep watching her as she ambles down the street. Near the end she stops to smell a flower on a bush, bringing it close to her nose; she turns to see if anyone is looking, puts her basket down, snaps the flower off and then continues. Turns left. I close the balcony doors, kneel down, and slide the seal of the cat flap to lock it.

Ivan has rung.

He said, "How are you?" and I said, "I'm fine."

His response was, "You sound a bit anxious."

I related the incident with George.

"Good," he said when I told him I had got him back. "And you are okay?"

"Yes, I'm fine."

"How fine—on a scale of one to ten?"

"Five point five."

This is the borderline mark, lower and he would come home.

"Are you sure?"

"Yes, I'm sure."

"You sound a bit breathless."

"What did you want, Ivan?"

There was a slight hesitation before he said, "I was just thinking of you."

I said nothing.

"You know it's you I really love, don't you?"

I hung up.

I am burning some frankincense; it makes breathing slower and deeper.

The courier says, "Delivery for Stella."

"Third floor," I say, and he comes up and I sign for the package.

The package: an expensive-looking white bag with bronzed braid handles, inside something of very little weight wrapped in white tissue, at the bottom of the bag a card. Ivan's handwriting. Evenly spaced capital letters. A manner of writing Ivan adopted for work to avoid misunderstandings.

SWEETHEART, PLEASE HAVE IT ON WHEN I GET HOME.

The color is purple, my bruise and the dress Ivan has had delivered to me. A knee-length slip made of silk, little spaghetti straps, bodice and hem trimmed with lace. The color is dark violet. It says so on the label that is still attached.

I put the dress on. I ring him.

"Was purple her favorite color?"

He says, "Yes."

He asks. "Does it fit?"

"Perfectly."

He adds, "You know it is you I really love."

"Is it?"

"Yes."

And he hangs up.

I sit in front of the computer in the dress he has sent me.

I make the search more precise. In the search box I type "Sophia Lawrence, Canada."

Nothing.

The purple of the dress accentuates the purple of the bruise. Maybe later there will be another bruise. The dress is dark violet. The bruise, aubergine.

I have been thinking as I have been filing.

Perhaps me in the purple dress will help him perform. May bring success to the occasion.

The situation. My suspicions. About Sophia and Ivan.

It's worse than I had first thought.

It was not that Sophia didn't let him.

It is that he never could. It was never a mission accomplished.

He was too overwhelmed at any opportunity. Too overwhelmed with desire. Too excited. A quivering wreck.

It is not that she didn't let him. It is that he loved her too much.

Ivan never had sex with Sophia. Because he couldn't. He loved her too much.

Ivan has never not been able to do the business with me.

He has never loved me as much as he loved her.

I imagine he will never love me as much as he loved her.

That sad smile I imagined she wore as she got up off the bed. Not coy refusal as I had thought.

"Don't you love me, Ivan? Is that what it is?"

She looks to the floor as she tucks her hair behind her ear. As she shifts her weight to one leg, the material of the purple dress she wears tightens over her thin hip. She places her hand on the same hip in preparation for his answer.

She asks him the question again. "Don't you love me, Ivan? Is that what it is?"

He still doesn't answer. He gets up off the bed, laces on his shoes, leaves the room.

I take the dress off and shake it over the bath, shower the particles away. I get dressed in my trousers and vest and put on my white coat. Wrap the bracelet back around my wrist. It has taken two emery boards to file the gold off the top edge of the bracelet. Two to file the bottom. Underneath the gold the metal is slate-colored and coarse.

"Hi, it's Stella again."

Ivan's mother greets me warmly.

"Do you know her married name?"

"Excuse me?"

"Sophia—her married name?"

She asks me to hold on. I can hear her open and close a drawer.

She comes back on the line. "Roberts—Sophia Roberts. . . . You really mustn't worry yourself. . . ."

"No, no—I'm not worried, just curious."

I thank her and put the phone down.

There is a Sophia Roberts who works in Neural Networking. Another who is an Olympic archer. Both of them are too young.

Purple: the color of poison.

It has not gone unnoticed: purple, the complementary color of yellow.

Red and blue—the color of my shoes.

Red and blue make purple.

These are the things that I think as I refold and restack the towels in the cupboard in the treatment room.

Mrs. O'Connor offers me a small smile but makes no comment about my appearance as I open the door. I find it a little disconcerting, her apparent disinterest. I touch my hair at the back of my head with the palm of my hand as she follows me down the passageway, in the hope it may prompt her to say something. She still says nothing.

"Do you think it suits me?" I ask her as I hand her the questionnaire.

She puts her questionnaire down on her lap and stares at me.

"It softens your features," she says finally. "You look more . . . bouncy."

"Bouncy?"

"Lighter."

She leans forward in her seat. Tilts her head to view me from a slightly different angle. She is about to say something about the swelling she can see.

"I had an accident, it's nothing to worry about."

"Oh . . . I'm sorry to hear that, Ms. Lewis. Marsha and Ann were concerned."

"Marsha and Ann?"

"Mrs. Toume and Mrs. Klein."

She explains to me how she just came from meeting with them. How they meet for coffee and cake once a week.

"We were wondering how it happened."

I relate the imagined incident with the medical cabinet. She smiles, puts her hand in front of her, lets out a small laugh.

I ask what is so funny.

"Ann—Mrs. Klein—thought perhaps you'd got drunk and fallen over. . . ."

Her gaze falls to the floor for a moment before she continues. "She said she could smell alcohol on your breath."

I inform her the "alcohol" is the brandy in the tincture I have been taking to calm the bruising. (*The tincture part is true. The reason for taking it is not. I have been taking valerian to help me stay relaxed.*)

My brusqueness has made her nervous. She stands up.

"Shall I get changed now?" She begins to walk behind the screen.

"Can I ask you another question?" I make sure my voice is tender.

She turns, looks puzzled but happy at my apparent sudden friendliness and willingness to communicate.

"What do you associate purple with?"

"Is this a test to see how I am?"

I tell her yes.

I sit on the chair in the passageway and wait for Mrs. O'Connor to change. She had closed her eyes, thought for a moment and then opened them. She said, "Passion." Not "Poison." She said, "Spirituality." Followed closely by, "Royalty." She seemed pleased with her answers.

Purple: it is not a color that has ever had any appeal to me.

"Has anything else been said about me?"

The fingers on Mrs. O'Connor's right hand twitch. Hardly perceptible, but I see it. She is lying on her front, her face pressed into the hole at the front of the table. I notice also how her breathing has quickened.

"No, no, not at all," she says.

I work her torso with firm strokes, slowly massage down her arms to her hands. I should have used a soft, less accusatory tone. Made her feel more comfortable about my inquiry. I know she is lying.

"I saw Mrs. Philips yesterday. She also has a bruise on her face," she tells me as I start to work on her fingers.

"Is that so?" I let the chimes tinkle away. I move to her other hand.

She relates to me what happened: After Mrs. Jones left here on Tuesday she went directly to Mrs. Philips's home.

Mrs. Philips opened the door; Mrs. Jones punched her, turned and left.

I made Mrs. Jones bolder than I intended. I am glad. I am also more sad than shocked. If I can make Mrs. Jones so bold I should be able to make myself have more courage.

I ask Mrs. O'Connor to turn over. She catches my eye, lifts herself to lean back on her elbows. "Mrs. Jones is very grateful to you," she says. "But it is a shame," she adds. "There'll be no more dinner parties at Mrs. Philips's for a while. She made a wonderful lemon syllabub. It was heavenly." Her eyes glide to the ceiling for a moment. She laughs a little. Stops. Looks at me straight in the face.

"Ms. Lewis, if we do talk about you, it's only because we are concerned—"

"Please lie down and close your eyes."

Mrs. O'Connor offers her hand as I open the door to see her out.

"We are all terribly fond of you. You make us all feel so much better."

I look at her hand suspended in midair, lift mine to meet it, feel her fingers squeeze around mine and release as if to confirm her sincerity. I look into her face, wait for my expected reaction to such displays of open emotion and her thinking that her seeming kindness can manipulate me into a possible friendship. I wait for the nausea to rise. The acidic taste in my mouth. The desire to vomit. Nothing. Nothing, because I have this sense deep inside that I am never going to see her again; there will be no conflict. There will be no problem. Yet I know this is ridiculous; she has booked an appointment for the same time next week.

I return her smile. Put it down to the blond hair. To Sophia seeping inside. To being more "bouncy," as she said I was.

I move onto the landing, watch her as she takes the stairs down.

She turns midway.

"See you next week," she says.

Behind Catrina Heksa's door I can hear a floorboard creak.

I turn, go back inside, double-lock the door.

Six o'clock: time for George to be fed. He leads the way to the cupboard where his food is kept, circles my feet, trills. As I open the cupboard, he lifts himself up onto his hind legs, slides his body against my leg, brushes his cheek against my knee. I stand for a while and watch him. He will keep doing this until I feed him. I bend, roll my trouser leg up to the knee. The brush of George's fur against the skin of my leg. It goes all the way to the heart, seems to still any anxiety there. *(Ivan thinks this ritual verges on unhealthy. He hasn't said so, but I sense it when he watches me. Sometimes I imagine he is jealous that he cannot produce the same pleasure he sees on my face.)* George does it twice more, gets impatient and paces away. I roll down the trouser leg. In the cupboard the tins are stacked height and depth according to flavor. Six varieties of flavor, all organic, recipes devised to circumvent the kidney conditions cats are prone to. I have read all about them on the Internet. I tried not to get sentimental. Tried not to make each kidney I read about one of George's kidneys. Today it is supposed to be "chicken" flavor. On the far right of the cupboard, a slender column of tins of sardines in olive oil. Portuguese—the best. They are also his favorite. I pull out a tin of the sardines.

"They are supposed to be for Sunday," I tell him as I open them.

I should have been more careful. It happened because I thought about Skye. Thought about the way she touched Ivan's neck. If he thought it was me, she would have touched him like I do. Moving her index finger from the dip at the base of his skull to about two inches down where his hair curls oddly to the right. Like the lid of the sardine tin did as I wound it open.

The cut is deep. But not deep enough to warrant stitches. Middle finger. Right hand. George is not happy; he has to wait while I tend to my wound, first with cold water, then a tea towel, then the tea tree cream and plasters ready in the drawer by the kitchen sink.

I watch George eat; I listen to the messages on the answerphone.

I rewind the tape, play the messages again.

Three messages:

The first is Skye. "Please call me when you get this."

The second is traffic noise.

The third is Ivan.

The second message should have been him too. He hadn't quite decided how to ask when he had rung the first time.

Had to put the phone down. The way he says it sounds as if he is ordering some special bit of equipment. Each word carefully pronounced. To avoid misunderstanding.

"Please wear dark lipstick."

It is less than an hour before he gets home.

"Coral" is the name given to the only lipstick I possess.

"Good afternoon, Ms. Lewis." The girl at the local pharmacy recognizes my voice.

"Good afternoon, Deirdre, I wonder if you could help me?"

She has promised to deliver via taxi, within fifteen minutes, a lipstick called "Raspberry." She offered to send another called "Myrtle."

"Please," I told her, "I'd rather not have the choice."

For a moment I go and stand in the passageway and listen: the hiss of gas is there. It is not as loud as I would expect it to be.

My conversation with Skye is brief.

"He has just left. . . . He was there for an hour. . . . He came out with two other men—an older man and a younger man, in suits . . . The gambler was there, too. They shook hands and then parted."

"Anything else?"

"No."

"I will call you later."

She rings back two minutes later.

"Are you sure you don't want me to come over?"

"No, I'm sure. I'll call you tomorrow."

"Or if anything happens," she adds.

She calls my name as I start to put down the receiver. "I forgot to ask—you rang earlier today. You left no message. That's not like you. What did you want?"

"I wanted to tell you about what Ivan said to me about yesterday. I changed my mind. I thought if I did, you'd get upset and you wouldn't go to the hotel."

She stays silent.

"Skye?"

"What?"

I relate Ivan's version of their meeting at the newsagent's; she listens without interruption. Waits a moment before she responds.

"Jesus, Stella—he's such a liar. He *wishes* I had touched his neck." Not a trace of anger in her voice. Only disappointment.

I could ask her what she means. About how he wishes she had touched his neck. I choose not to.

She clears her throat, lights a cigarette. She smokes far too much. "I should come around—we should sort this out."

"No—I'll call you tomorrow." I put the receiver gently back into its cradle.

The taxi driver says, "Ms. Lewis, delivery for you."

I buzz him in, wait for him on the landing.

I exchange the five-pound note for the small paper bag he hands me, tell him to keep the change. He holds the note up to the skylight, examines it from both sides and tells me, as he takes his wallet from his back pocket, "You have to be careful these days." He places the note neatly inside and thanks me as he takes the stairs down. As I turn to move inside, something changes on Catrina Heksa's door. A very small change. Something changing from dark to light on the white expanse. Toward the top. Like a smudge of dirt has suddenly been cleaned. Like a small beam of light has appeared. I hear the creak of a floorboard behind her door. I go inside, close my door. Look through my peephole out onto the empty landing and to her door. Notice again a change on her door. This time her peephole changes from light to dark. She is checking to see I have gone inside. I will wait until it changes from dark to light again, and then I will move away. I stare out onto the empty landing and her door.

I now know how she knew I had red hair before I ever saw her.

It is nearly a minute until she moves away. I counted.

I feel: bemused she should be so interested, relieved someone is more paranoid than me, happy someone else is guarding the territory, angry that she is so nosy, sorry for her because she feels the need. Because perhaps she is lonely. I have been there too.

Maybe, like me, she is always in a state of anticipation.

Maybe, like me, she is waiting for Ivan to come home.

If he has left the hotel, he should be on his way home.

He will be home soon.

I have undressed and washed. The purple dress is ready, hanging on the back of the bathroom door. There are still some gold filings on it from earlier. I shake them off, slip the dress over my head and straighten the thin straps. It is the sort of dress with which no underwear should be worn. I brush the ash blond hair and tuck the few red strands that have escaped back under the wig with a hairpin. I apply the flesh-colored concealer to the bruise. Add the translucent powder. I am not sure what else to do with my eyes. I smear Vaseline on the lids to make them shine and on the lashes to make them transparent. I apply the lipstick carefully with a fine brush. The color of the Raspberry lipstick is a dark red-blue. Like the color of blood with no oxygen in it. The contrast makes me look paler. Brings out the green of her/my eyes. I stare at my reflection. There is something of the insect about me now. That is what I think. I want to think "butterfly," but it does not seem quite right. I blot the lipstick with tissue, powder and reapply. It comes to me. Ladybird. Not quite the right colors. But that is the impression. I am not unhappy with the association. Bright, cheerful, friendly with an edge of the sinister, which is what makes it alluring. I smile. I run my tongue along my lips. The lipstick has been flavored with the fruit it is named after. I put on the shoes, the ones with the marabou trim.

In the treatment room, I select a scent that I think would be "Sophia." I think of snow and choose peppermint. Fresh. Invigorating and cooling. I look at myself again in the mirror above the sink and put the bottle of peppermint back in the cabinet. I remove the frankincense, patchouli, rose otto, spikenard, vetiver and ylang-ylang. I base my choices on the assumption that those women who like purple gravitate toward fragrances that are musty, spicy, exotic or sweet; Sophia has suddenly moved from "West" to "East." On a broomstick. Hair and gown horizontal on the breeze.

I wait for Ivan in the kitchen. I could wait in the bedroom but I don't want to make it that easy for him. I am imagining his smile. I am not sure whether to smile or not.

The scent of the patchouli is heavy and musky and weaving its way through the flat.

Ivan is late.

George moves again from my feet to sit by the locked cat flap. He sighs. I turn to him. Again I say, "No." He blinks and comes back to nuzzle my feet. He has been doing this dance for the last fifteen minutes.

At the front door, the knocking is gentle but persistent. She calls out, "Sophia—Sophia, are you there?" I have the feeling she will keep calling it until I open the door. Catrina Heksa knows I am in. I am always in.

If I don't answer the door, she may meet Ivan on the landing. Perhaps this is her intention. Perhaps she has been keeping a timetable.

I open the door.

Catrina Heksa is no longer wearing her scarf and her hair is black. Her hair is black as the night. But softly layered. Shoulder length. Her tan has built to a pale bronze.

"Hello."

"Hello."

"Sorry to disturb you—I just wanted to . . ."

"Yes?"

She opens up the small bag she is carrying, lifts from it a fake white mouse, its eyes beady and pink, places it in the palm of her hand.

"A present—a belated apology . . . for asking you to take off the bells. . . ."

I look at the mouse in her hand. It looks like it has already been mauled. She stretches her hand out. I make no move.

"I think he's asleep right now," I tell her.

She glances over my shoulder. I turn my head, follow her gaze: George sliding sexily against the wall as he makes his way toward us.

Her kissing noise is not like mine. Higher pitched. Closer to a squeak. But it is effective; his patter quickens. I catch him, scoop him up as he reaches my feet, hold him close to my chest.

"Hi, Kitty," she says.

She reaches her free hand across, rubs the space in front of his ear. He leans his head into her hand. She squints her eyes. George squints back. She knows all the tricks. How to make friends with a cat. She dangles the mouse in front of his face. He bats it playfully as she throws me a quick glance.

"How's the face?"

"It's fine, thank you."

"And your hand?" She looks at the plasters on my fingers.

"It's nothing." I look at the floor. She is wearing the white sandals. I look up again. She increases the swing of the mouse. Smiles. I am not sure if it is just friendly or knowing.

George has stretched out his paws. We watch him as he maneuvers the head of the mouse into his mouth.

"He is such a darling."

"Yes, he is."

"And such good company."

"Yes."

My eyes drift again to the floor. She does not seem to keep her feet still. Her right foot moves alternately to being parallel with her left, to bringing the heel of it to the left's toes. Now she rests the heel of her right foot on top of her left foot and leans on the frame of the doorway.

She smiles at me again; she is waiting for me to invite her in. "My husband works in the service industry."

"I'm sorry, I don't understand."

"He works in hotels . . . out early, back late, sometimes not back at all."

She moves back up to standing upright, her right foot has taken a step over the threshold. "Are you busy?" She eyes my purple dress. My marabou shoes.

"I'm expecting Ivan any moment."

"You look very nice—he's lucky he has someone who bothers to dress up for him. . . ."

I say what I've wanted to say since I opened the door. "Your hair—is it natural?"

She lets go of the mouse, leans forward to kiss George on his head. Her head near my shoulder, I focus in on her roots. Note the tiny edge of gray the hairdresser has overlooked. She stands, moves her right leg back in line with her left, stares me full in the face.

"Is anything natural?" In different circumstances I might engage in this discussion. Her eyes flick for a moment up to my hairline, then back to my face. "Always good to have a change—variety is the spice of life and all that."

"Quite," is all I can think of to say. The first time in my life I have used the word like this. The lady in agreement. The lady who does not want to enter into discussion but wants to remain polite.

"Maybe next time, then. Coffee. It would be nice to get to know you better."

She bends at her knees. Lowers herself so her eye line is with George's. "See you later, Kitty." The same voice I heard the other night while emptying the rucksack. The one that sounds like she is consoling a child. George was with her then. It has been going on for some time.

George is chewing the mouse's head. He looks up at Catrina Heksa and blinks. They have a thing going; it is obvious. I squeeze him a little tighter to me.

"Well, better let you get on then."

"Yes."

She turns; I watch her take the few steps that are needed to get to her door, which she has left ajar. I watch her go in, and I close my door. George struggles to get out of my arms. I let him down into the passageway. He stays by the front door. Meows.

Things are not the way they should be at all.

In the kitchen I open another tin of sardines. Scoop them out into his bowl. I surround the bowl with pinches of catnip.

I call him with my kissing noise. I stroke his back while he eats.

Ivan should be home by now.

···

"Where are you?"

"I'm in the van."

"Where?"

"Outside."

"Why?"

"I wanted to be sure you were ready."

"I am."

"Are you wearing the dress?"

"Yes."

"Are you wearing the lipstick?"

"Yes—it tastes of raspberry."

"I'm going to knock on the door three times."

"Okay."

"But you mustn't let me in straightaway"

"What do you mean?"

"Wait until I knock again."

"Ivan?"

"What?"

"Can I smile at you?"

"I'd rather you didn't."

He puts the phone down.

Down below in the street I can hear him as he opens and then closes the door of his van.

I stand in the center of the passageway and wait.

I should have known it would happen.

He knocked three times. He waited. He must have counted to a hundred, as I did. He knocked again. I put my hand on the lock and was about to open the door. And then I heard another door opening and Catrina Heksa's voice.

"She's definitely in—I just saw her."

I should have known it had the potential for farce.

I press my ear against the door. If I open the door, the mood will be broken. I feel like the bride who mustn't be seen before the right moment. It will be bad luck.

"It's to warn her I'm coming in. Her clients get nervous if they suddenly see a man." He talks fast. He is impatient.

"She wasn't wearing her white coat—I don't think she has any clients. I'm Catrina, by the way. You must be Ivan?"

Through the peephole I can see him turn and shake her hand.

"Nice to meet you."

Her eyes drift down his body and hover for a second at that part of his body. What I am imagining is confirmed by her nervous smile. Ivan has an erection. He has probably been trying to quell it all day.

"I just remembered something. Can you hold on a second? One second, I promise," she says. She holds up one finger. Smiles a little too sweetly.

I watch her as she steps inside her front door and then out again onto the landing. She has in her hand the flower I saw her pick earlier.

"I meant to give it to . . ." She hesitates. She says, "Stella." *(She has been talking to the caretaker.)*

The flower is a rose. The color of apricots. Rude in its tight bud, threatening to burst open. She hands it to Ivan.

"I'd better not keep you," she says with suggestion.

She looks at the door as she says this. At the peephole. As Ivan is turning she winks. The wink is for me, not him.

Ivan turns back to the door. He looks neither angry nor bemused nor embarrassed. He is not really experiencing the moment. He is elsewhere. He turns the first lock.

"Have a nice evening," she says.

If her flat has a malevolent spirit, let it take her now.

I did not wait for him in the passageway. Before he pushed the door open, I slipped into the bedroom and closed the door. So he could knock again. We could still do what he wanted.

But he didn't bother to knock. He came straight in. I was sitting on the bed.

"Stand up," he said. I stood up.

"Come over here." I walked over to him.

We stood opposite each other and he glanced me up and down. His face expressionless. Beads of sweat on his forehead, accumulating in the vertical crease. I lifted my hand to wipe them away. Shouldn't have done that. He caught my wrist. I flinched because I thought he was going to hit me.

"Don't be silly," he whispered. He brought my hand back down to my side.

"Walk over to the window." His breathing was getting deeper. I could see the buttonholes on the front of his shirt stretch.

Ten steps are what it took.

"Turn around. Walk back to me."

As I walked he moved toward the wardrobe, toward the panel with the full-length mirror.

"To me. To me," he said. *(I had been walking in a straight line, back to my original position.)*

"I want you to come and stand here." He pointed at the floor in front of the mirror.

I stood there and lifted my arms above my head. I thought it would help him to take the dress off.

He shook his head. I put my arms down. He came and stood behind me, put his hands on my bare shoulders, motioned me forward, closer to the mirror. His hands were damp; when he took them away the wet they left grew cold very quickly.

He put his hand in the middle of my shoulder blades, pushed so I had to lean forward. I put my palms on the icy surface of the mirror. I caught his eye in the reflection, grew suddenly shy and averted my gaze. He brought his hand around to the side of my face and moved it back.

"Look at me. I want you to look at me all the time."

With the toe of his foot, he tapped my ankles so I would move my feet wider apart. To hip width.

He leaned slightly against me to undo his trousers and then he lifted up the back of the dress.

The act was over for him almost as soon as it had begun. It was neither gentle nor rough. It had about it the quality of placing an object very carefully and purposely on a table. With complete mindfulness. Silent. Noiseless.

I had looked at him as he had asked. He had closed his eyes. There was a moment when his skin became almost luminescent. His face looked like a peaceful saint you see in paintings.

And then the deed was done and it had faded.

He moved away so I could stand. He held me very tight under the dress, his arms around my waist, his face pressed into the back of my head. As I made to go, to release myself from his grasp, his hands went to my hips, and his nails—he has long nails—dug in. I pushed my elbow back against his body. I could feel under my elbow the hardness of a rib.

He moved his head, looked at me in the reflection. It wasn't quite a smile he gave me. It was a mouth shape somewhere between gratitude and guilt. His grip loosened. I brought my elbow forward, away from his ribs.

We did not look at each other as I left the room.

The rose Mrs. Heksa had given him to give to me was lying on the passageway floor. I picked it up and took it to the kitchen and put it in a glass of water.

In the bathroom I washed and applied tea tree to the crescent-shaped marks on my hips. One of them had drawn blood. I reapplied my lipstick even though it did not need reapplying.

I tied the hair back in preparation for cooking dinner.

Ivan went into the living room and turned on the television.

I have set our plates side by side so we do not have to look at each other. Usually I set them opposite to each other. Ivan makes no comment as he sits down. He takes a pinch of salt and sprinkles it onto his food.

We both take a forkful of okra and rice. Chew slowly. Swallow. Repeat the process until our plates are clean. We line up our cutlery on our plates.

We look at each other for the first time.

"You cut another finger?"

"Yes."

He glances at the locked cat flap and the closed balcony doors and at the fake white mouse that lies nearby. At George who has taken to sleeping by the locked cat flap. He looks again at the mouse.

"New toy?"

"The woman you met on the landing gave it to him; she is trying to steal him."

He gives me his look. His "take a reality check" look. Nothing discernible. Not that anyone else would notice. A tensing of the muscles in his upper cheeks.

He calls George. We watch him stand, stretch and yawn and patter over. Ivan lifts him onto his lap, rubs his head with his knuckles.

"Is she the one who gave you the letter?"

"She said she didn't look inside."

Ivan concentrates on the tips of George's ears. Rubbing them in between his finger and thumb.

"Is it a long relationship you've had with this man—this gambler person?" I ask him.

Only his eyes move up to look at me. He puts George down onto the floor, gets up, clears the table. Behind me I can hear him as he puts the plates into the sink. Then I can feel his hands in my hair, loosening it from the band I had tied it up with to cook. He tidies the hair around my shoulders. Strokes it from crown to shoulder on both sides. He does this twice.

"I thought you said, 'No questions.'"

"This is different—I saw the letter."

"He is an old friend," he says.

He has told me in the past he has no friends. I am his only friend. I tell him this.

"I have one or two, Miss Moneypenny."

"I don't think you should call me 'Miss Moneypenny' when I'm wearing the wig. I think 'Sophia' would be more appropriate."

I feel the pressure of his lips on the top of my head. "You are a strange one," he says.

"No stranger than you," I reply.

He squeezes my shoulders and moves away.

I asked him if there was anything about me, anything natural, that was in any way like Sophia. He stared at me for a little while. He offered me that there was possibly something in the shape of my profile and the way I have of looking over my shoulder to talk to him when my back is turned.

"But nothing else?"

His smile was wry. "The way you talk . . . the sound of your voice is exactly like hers."

I smiled back. I said nothing more.

I got up and lifted a plate from the washing-up rack and dried it.

Ivan that first day in my doorway. My gallant knight.

"Please, come in," I had said and he suddenly leaned on the doorframe. It wasn't the cool macho actorly gesture I had thought it was. He had been swooning. He had heard my voice, gone weak at the knees. He needed to lean against the doorframe to keep his balance. Or to confirm his luck.

I look at him as he rinses the knives and forks under the tap. I should be angry. I am thinking more how glad I am that Skye's voice is nothing like mine. Which means it is nothing like Sophia's. It was Skye's voice that seduced Tim. I am sure of it. Tim used to find it sexy when I got a cough or sore throat. He would melt.

"Talk to me—talk to me . . ." he would say.

The male commentator's voice is flirty and seductive. He spreads his arms wide to emphasize the size of the beach he stands on. The camera tracks back. He walks toward the camera. He says the sea around the island is renowned for its attraction to scuba divers. Weekly courses are available for beginners. He picks up a handful of the sand that is white and lets it fall through his fingers. There is a sunset. There is a palm tree; its leaves quiver in the breeze.

"It is like paradise," he says. Off camera. In the background.

He says the name of the island again.

Ivan and I sit as we normally do of an evening, at either end of the sofa. Legs crossed, our hands meeting in the middle in the slight gap of the cushions. George is curled asleep to my right, one paw resting on my leg.

Ivan and I have not said a word to each other since sitting down. Since putting on the television. This in itself is not uncommon. Except tonight the silence feels nervous rather than comfortable.

The program credits roll onto the screen.

Ivan leans over, places his hand on my thigh. It feels warm through the purple silk of the dress. I am aware that there is an overfriendliness to this gesture. It feels forced. Like his smile.

"Shall I run you a bath?"

"Say, 'Shall I run you a bath, Sophia?'"

He rubs at his eye. Stares at me. Winks at me with his green eye.

"Shall I run you a bath, Sophia?"

"Say it without a Scottish accent," I tell him.

He does. Her name from his mouth is like an arrow. My blood rises up to meet it.

I kiss him on the cheek. "Thank you, Ivan, that would be very nice."

While I take my nightly bath is the time he says he sorts out his jacket pockets. Tonight I listen more closely and hear the crinkling of his nylon jacket, the creak of his knees as he bends down, the hush of material against the wooden floor, the sound of a long zip, the slide of paper against paper, the zip again as he does it up. When he has finished, he comes in to wash my back as he always does. There is the usual joke about pushing George, who sits on the corner of the bath, into the water. When Ivan first moved in, he didn't bother sorting out his jacket pockets.

I took off the wig to have the bath, replaced it once I got out and dried myself. Ivan stood in the bathroom doorway watching. I put in my green eyes. I put on the purple dress. My marabou slippers. A smile passed between us.

The sex started off tender, soft caresses to my neck and my face, my shoulders, my arms, kissing my fingers, the palms of my hands. Kneeling down, he lifted the front of the dress, stuck out his tongue and leaned forward. Began to lick and probe. But not for very long. Not for long enough. He stood up, took hold of my wrists, stared at me. He said very softly, "I want you to pretend like you don't want me to. Okay?"

We stared at each other; I stayed perfectly still.

"Okay," I said. "Is that what she did?" I asked.

His smile was obscene. His smile was pornographic.

"She liked it like that," he said. His hand tightened around my wrist. He moved forward, so I had to step back. He pinned me against the bathroom wall with his weight.

"Resist me," he said.

He slowly leaned more weight onto me. Pressed his full weight against me. I struggled. It began. I hit him. I bit him. I pulled his hair. I scratched his face. I made my legs rigid, held them close together. He caught my hands, dragged my arms up, over my head. Held them there, pressed his groin into mine. His breath fast and deep, his eyes wide, his nostrils flaring. I could feel his other hand force itself between my thighs. I pressed them tighter together. He made a deft move. His hand suddenly moving around my waist and into the small of my back, his foot at my ankles, sweeping my feet forward so I slid down the tiles and onto the floor.

I played the game, tried to escape, turning onto my front, crawling out the door.

He let me crawl to halfway down the passageway; I turned my head back to see him watching.

The next thing I knew, I was being caught at the knees, being turned, being held down. A hand around my throat, being told, "Don't move."

His other hand inside the dress, slowly touching and smoothing, describing an arabesque, but the pressure changing from light to heavy to rough.

Dress being pulled up, his trousers being unzipped. His movements frantic.

And then he was in. And then as if invisible strings pulled at his skin, it tightened across his face; he didn't look like himself. "Sophia," he said as he arched his back, and it was over. He fell loosely onto me. Limbs limp. We stayed like that until his breathing evened and quietened, me stroking the back of his neck, the space between his shoulders. He got up, helped me up, smoothed my hair, kissed my hands and my palms. The tops of each shoulder. My forehead.

"Shall we go to bed?" he said.

He led me by the hand to the bedroom. We undressed slowly, got into bed, the only noise between us the hush of the cotton sheets against each other and our skin. His body got hotter as he fell asleep.

Ivan's jacket makes a noise even if you breathe on it. I hold it close to my body. Take it into the kitchen, close the door.

Side pocket, left-hand side: A red pen and a black pen. A group of receipts held together with a paper clip.

Side pocket, right-hand side: Wallet—one credit card, a ten-pound note. The receipt for the purple dress (*one hundred sixty-five pounds—paid in cash*). Loose in the pocket, three one-pound coins. A twenty-pence piece. A packet of Juicy Fruit gum. His front-door keys, a key ring that is a bottle opener in the shape of a shark. His car keys.

It is good to see he separates his left and right to business and personal.

Inside pocket right: one valid passport. The picture is recent, the date of issue one month ago. Another car key I have not seen before.

Inside pocket left: one mobile phone. The address book in the mobile phone has only one name in it, and it is mine. I check the numbers he has rung during the course of the day. There are seven. Four are mine: the call to tell me he was thinking of me, the messages to tell me about the dark lipstick, including the one where he didn't speak, the call from the van to see if I was ready.

Two of the other three numbers are the same.

I dial the number.

The woman at the other end of the line says, "The Charles Hotel, can I help you?"

"Sorry, wrong number," I tell her.

The other number is a mobile. It was rung at 3:22; the call lasted five minutes.

I dial the number. The woman clears her throat.

"Hi, Ivan—is something wrong? It's very late." A woman's voice. Skye's voice.

The back of the phone falls off as it hits the floor.

I hid the passport in the same place I hid the photographs, beneath the loose floorboard under the kitchen table. I hung the jacket back where it was. Third peg to the left of the front door.

Tonight the money in the rucksack is foreign. Deutschmarks, francs, pesos, lire, yen and dollars. The notes soft with use. The denominations vary.

In the bottom layer of his toolbox, a run of slender cardboard cylinders. I removed one, slid out the curl of paper and unrolled it. An antique map. Beside the cylinders three scalpels carefully sheathed and a computer disk.

I took the computer disk to the living room, turned on the computer.

I could open the disk, but I couldn't open what was on there. "Unrecognized file type" came up each time I clicked on any of the files.

I notice it as I walk down the passageway to put the disk back in the toolbox. I have started to limp. My body knows I may have to go soon. Go out there.

. . .

I have opened the document on the computer entitled "Procedure to Get Out." It is a very old document. (I have read the relevant books, seen the task lists to self-recovery. The reality checks . . . I am not stupid. . . . *I have devised strategies.*)

> landing outside front door to second-floor landing
> landing outside front door to first-floor landing
> landing outside front door to black and white tiles
> landing outside front door to main front door
> all above stages and then
> open main front door
> open main front door and walk down stone steps
> open main front door and walk down stone steps and
>   to the end of the path
> open main front door and walk down stone steps and
>   to the end of the path and turn left onto pavement
>   and walk to first lamppost
> and then all stages to second lamppost
> and then all stages to third lamppost
> and then all stages to end of street and turn left

The last time I tried to go out, just before I met Ivan, Skye was in the flat; she had promised me she would not leave George alone. Whatever happened. I got as far as the black and white tiles. Then a panic attack seized me. The caretaker had to help me. He held my rucksack in one hand, and with the other he guided me back up the stairs.

Things have changed; George no longer loves me only. Neither does Ivan. Neither does Skye.

In the kitchen George is scratching at the cat flap. He turns his head to look at me as I walk in. Meows. I kneel down, unlock the cat flap, watch his tail get caught in the flap as it comes down, as it always does. Through the glass I see him turn right. Very faintly I hear Catrina Heksa's voice say, "Hi, Kitty."

I open the balcony doors, go out on the balcony. The air smells damp and slightly floral. It is late, nearly dawn; there are still a few lights on in the other houses. And in the tower blocks in the distance. I watch as one car makes its way from one end of the street to the other.

As I am walking down the passageway to the front door, I sniff the air. Turn my head left and right. I stop.

It should be overwhelming, the smell of gas. It is not there at all.

I look at my reflection in the mirror, readjust the wig so the part sits straight. I look at my bare feet, debate for a moment if I should wear shoes; it would mean going into the bedroom. It could mean Ivan may wake. May ask questions: *"Where have you been? What are you doing?"* I could ask him the same.

The rucksack is heavy. The weight pulls at my shoulders. The straps dig in. I look at the front door. There are three locks to be undone. I turn the first key as quietly as I can, hear the metal sliding. A clunk as it releases. I check the bedroom door. Wait to hear if Ivan is stirring. Nothing. I stand closer to the door, hoping my body will muffle the sound as I turn the next key. I check the bedroom door again before I turn the last. I open the door, slowly pull it to behind me. It makes the slightest clink.

On the landing the lino is cold underfoot. Colder under the toes, where the metal strip of the top step digs in its dips and grooves. I imagine its imprint. Deep by now: I have been standing like this for a while, watching the frosted-glass window at the foot of the stairs, at the edge of the mini landing, get lighter.

The building is creaking around me. Tiny creaks. Things are warming up. I can hear my breathing. As I am breathing in, I am imagining the air going up my spine. As I am breathing out, I am imagining it like a waterfall falling inside my face, inside my ribs and my hips and then under; it is ready then to breathe in again. I read in a book somewhere that this sort of breathing is supposed to keep one calm. My right hand is getting clammy against the banister, the fingers throbbing underneath their plasters. The air is very still, apart from my breath, which I can see out of the corner of my eye is making some strands of hair move. I can smell disinfectant and floor polish. A faint touch of oregano. Someone must have cooked Italian.

A moment ago water moving down a drainpipe.

I tuck my hair behind my ear; it will untuck again as I take a step, and I will have to tuck it behind my ear again. I take the first two steps. Watch my feet that don't look like my feet. Glance at my hand as it slides on the banister and the trail of sweat it leaves. I take two more steps. I count to six. I'm on the mini landing. I stay holding the banister; it guides me right into the corner, along the side of the window, around the corner. Dust has collected underneath my feet, felting them. A tiny bit of grit is grinding just on the inside of my second toe. I stop, use a finger to remove it. Ten more steps in front of me. Twenty more to go.

I whisper the numbers as I go. The metal strip against my toes like a confirmation. The lace hem of the purple dress flicking at my knees.

Ten more steps. Second-floor landing. I look at the numbers on the doors as I pass. I have never talked to the people who live behind them. I have only ever seen them once or twice. And even then I can't be sure who lives where.

Ten more steps. Another window. Another corner. Another bit of grit. In the other foot this time. I wipe it on the side of my leg. Note the smudge of dirt that is left.

The rucksack has suddenly grown heavier. I readjust the straps and then continue.

Ten more steps. First-floor landing. Two more doors. I have noticed I have increased my pace. I slow down again. Take the steps as a child would. Bringing one foot to rest by the other on the step before commencing the next. The last window. It is growing lighter by the minute. The air is not as grainy as it was. I can see the flecked pattern in the lino. Gray and white and gold. The gray, dots as if someone has spilled pepper. Like the grainy air has just fallen. I have stopped in the corner by the window. Around the next bend, I will be able to see the main front door. My heart knows. Moves a bit faster. I fumble in the side pocket of the rucksack, find the

Rescue Remedy, open it, tilt my head back and administer five drops, put it back. Do a little more of the breathing. Let the banister guide me around. Slide my foot against and down the step.

One. Two. Three. Four. Five. Six. Seven. Eight. Nine. Ten.

It is suddenly colder; the black and white tiles are icy underfoot. Seem to draw all the heat from my body like a plumb line straight down inside me.

I am keeping to the white tiles. There is no reason. My feet slap softly against them.

I run my fingers along the gray metal post boxes that lead to the main front door.

Old-fashioned. Black. Wide as two normal doors. An arch window at its top. The first shadows falling. The lock is old too. A handle that has to be grabbed and pulled toward you. There is a gap between the lock and the hold large enough to be able to see the mechanism slide back.

I lift my hand.

I faint.

I don't know how long I am out for. I don't know where I am at first when I come to. The caretaker is looking down at me. Softly calling my name. He guides me back up the stairs. He asks no questions. He waits on the landing until I close the door.

Right knee, left knee and then right elbow. I rub on the arnica ointment in the order of impact.

Ivan does not wake as I crawl into bed.

SATURDAY

Ivan has to peel my orange for me—the cuts on my fingers have turned septic and swollen. He divides the orange, pulls apart the segments, puts them on my plate. I will wait until he has done the same with his orange before I start to eat.

We eat and sip at our glasses of water. We will continue in silence until the oranges are vanished, the glasses of water empty. Every time I pick up my glass, the bracelet walks down my arm and clanks against the side of the glass. The note it makes getting progressively higher. He glances at me, eyes only shifting in his head, each time it happens.

Ivan has put music on. Disco. I think he has done this to avoid conversation. Or to try to keep the mood light. Earlier, as he peeled my orange for me, he sang along with a chorus.

I think he used to dance with her to this song.

He woke me this morning to have sex.

The acid of the orange stings the skin around my lips.

The skin feels raw from Ivan kissing me so much. So passionately. Underneath the wig my head is starting to itch. It feels like perhaps an army of insects is breeding under there.

I have the feeling there will not be a time of oranges again. Things have slipped—are slipping somewhere else. I have burned geranium to help keep the mood light.

I follow him into the passageway, give him the shopping list, and he kisses me good-bye at the front door.

"I love you," he says.

"I love you, too."

On the landing he turns and smiles. "You look very beautiful."

The pitch of his voice just so; it is neither sickening flattery nor false. It is charming. It makes me blush.

He turns again, and I close the door, walk to the balcony, wave as he drives away.

Before, he has referred to me as handsome. As attractive. It is the first time he has called me beautiful. In the passageway I smile at myself in the mirror. I turn away to take the wig off; I do not want to see Stella today. I scratch my head. Put the wig back on. Turn again to set it straight.

Tonight when he comes home, I will make sure the music he put on this morning will be playing.

The money in the rucksack has gone. He must have got up while I was still sleeping. Transferred it to his pockets. Or to an envelope. In his drawer of the chest, underneath the paper that lines it, three manila letter-size envelopes. The type with the gusset so it can expand.

142   I sit on the bed. I would like to lie down and sleep. The

waves of tiredness are coming now at regular intervals. But it is too late to ring my morning clients; they are also two of the clients I canceled from Wednesday. It would be unfair; I am not completely uncaring. The waves of tiredness are competing with the waves of itchiness under the wig. I keep slipping my hand underneath to scratch. I keep closing my eyes; my body feels like it is falling. I stand up, drag the sheets and covers over the bed; my fingers are too sore to make the bed with my usual careful precision, with its tight hospital corners. It is a shame; I would like to see the clean cut of a diagonal. I would find it comforting.

I have rung the pharmacy, ordered two packets of ash blond hair dye and a box of over-the-counter pills to help keep me awake.

"Did you like the Raspberry lipstick?" Deirdre asked.

"Yes, it is very nice," I told her.

I ring the two clients that are booked for the afternoon, rearrange their appointments, telling them I am ill; they wish me better, hope it is nothing serious.

I ring Skye.

"Can you come at one?" I ask her.

"I can be there at three," is her reply.

She adds, "You sound anxious."

"I'm fine," I tell her.

"Laters," she says as she hangs up.

I have refolded all the towels in the cupboard in the treatment room. I have turned all the bottles so the labels and names are exactly centered. I called for George, making the kissing noise, but he didn't come.

I put on my blue shoes.

Things are never going to be as they were.

Every cell in my body is telling me this.

My first client is Mrs. Lofthouse. I nod my greeting as I open the door, lead her down the passageway into the treatment room, hand her the questionnaire and a freshly sharpened pencil.

"I like the hair," she says.

"Thank you."

"Are you better now?"

"I'm fine." I am lying.

I feel one degree away from collapse. The pills I have taken have induced a mild shivering. I check her questionnaire. I leave her to change.

I keep my injured fingers from contact by using only my palm. Use my left hand as much as I can. Mrs. Lofthouse does not seem to notice the difference. I focus on each moment. Concentrate on the texture of her skin, the wideness and depth of her pores, the way the flesh moves as my hands move across, the viscosity of the oil, the mixed aroma of juniper and orange. I listen to the chimes going from high to low. I sink into the pain in my fingers as I forget for a moment that they are sore, using them to press in the base of her back. I don't want to think. I don't want to debate the questions and thoughts that keep rising to the surface.

My failure to get out last night.

That I don't care what Ivan is up to. As long as he doesn't leave.

That I should be strong and ask him to leave.

That I have never really loved him. Not like Tim. Or even like George.

That this has just been a convenience. Me and him.

That this is a lie.

That I no longer know what to think.

That I no longer know who I am.

That these thoughts are not unfamiliar.

That I should go with the flow.

That I don't like the flow.

That I don't know what "flow" is.

Except for a brief moment when I used to run hurdles.

An image of Skye floats into the thoughts like seaweed in water.

The memory of her voice: *"Hi, Ivan—is something wrong?—It's very late."*

I see Mrs. Lofthouse out. Return to the treatment room. Throw the used towel into the dirty laundry. Replace the paper on the table. Straighten the bottles. Clean the bowls. Sharpen the pencil. Lay out a fresh questionnaire. I keep busy until Mrs. Boyle arrives. I refold the fresh towels again. Pile them accurately. I go into the kitchen. Stare for a while at the girl on the packet of the hair dye. Eyes too blue. Smile too bright. Future promising. I read the instructions in the hair-dye kit. Out loud. Just under my breath. I take another tablet to keep me awake. I check that the bruise on my face is concealed. Reapply lipstick.

Mrs. Boyle, like her name, sweats. Her skin is naturally greasy. The repulsion I feel is a welcome distraction.

"Thank you," I tell her as she leaves.

I watch her from the balcony as she walks down the street and turns left.

There are three messages on the answerphone. They always seem to come in threes. The first message is from Ivan's mother.

She wants me to know she'd got her years mixed up with the Christmas cards. The card she had looked at, the one from Sophia that said she was getting divorced, it was the Christmas before last. She had found the card, the one from last year. Sophia has got remarried to a computer programmer called Dirk. She and he, and her two kids from the previous marriage, they all live in a wood cabin by a lake.

"I hope I have put your mind at ease," she said.

The information is interesting but no longer relevant.

The second and the third messages are both blank. The caller seemed to hesitate before putting the phone down.

I rang Ivan's mother back to thank her for taking the trouble to call me. To tell her I was grateful. I got more than I bargained for.

"I thought it would make you a little less worried," she said.

"Yes, yes, it has," I reassured her.

There was a pause.

"Is something wrong with Ivan's phone?" she asked. "I can't seem to get through."

"I haven't rung him today," I told her. "Do you phone him often?" I added.

"Every day," she said.

"Did you tell him that I spoke with you?"

I think she could detect by my tone that if she had, I would rather she had not.

She was quiet.

"Stella, if I have caused trouble I am sorry. I felt it important he knew about your concern."

"Yes. Indeed. Quite." I heard myself say the words twice.

"Did he tell you about Canada? I told him he should tell you about Canada."

"He has not elaborated—no—I have not asked him to," I told her.

Her voice took on a sympathetic tone. "Stella—it was only a minor offense—you must not judge him too much. 'Canada'—it is the word we use for 'prison.'"

I was standing. I sat down.

"It was her fault—he forged the money to pay for the ticket. It was very expensive in those days to travel."

I wondered if I should tell her he has now mastered his art. No longer gets caught out.

147

"Is he as generous to you as he is to me?" she said.

She knew already.

"Do not judge him too much," she said again before she put down the phone.

I dial Ivan's number. He picks up immediately.

"Ivan?"

The phone line goes silent. Comes back to life. Dies again.

(Last night, when I dropped the phone, I think I must have broken it.)

The itching, it was getting unbearable. I have mixed up the hair-dye solution and put on the see-through polythene gloves. I look at the picture of the girl on the front of the packet. Her blue eyes and bright smile full of encouragement. I take off the wig, place my right hand behind my back to stop me from using it, tip my head over the kitchen sink. Work from back to front as per the instructions.

I comb through the dye sitting at the kitchen table, head bent forward. As I coil the hair on top of my head I notice under the table a fleck of wood lighter than its surround. A shard missing from one of the loose floorboard's narrow edges. It was not like that last night.

Fetching a knife from the kitchen drawer, I crawl under the table. Lift up the floorboard.

I look at the kitchen door. At its keyhole. Imagine Ivan's eye behind it last night watching me.

There is no passport.

There are no photographs.

I think about the way he made love to me this morning; the peculiarity of his smile, which I thought was to do with pleasure; the way his hands were wrapped tightly around my wrists. I think about the way he called me "beautiful" as he left.

I look into the dark space; he probably thinks what I did is charming. He is probably flattered. Or he has put it down to my "illness." Along with the phone calls to his mother.

I am not the only one with an illness. We are well suited. Perhaps he thinks he has found his match. This is what I think as I open the bedside drawer looking for the cigar box. The drawer is empty. Ivan has been busy. No doubt he thinks it has served its purpose.

I heat a needle over the gas flame, watch it go orange and then white. Wait for it to cool, slip it under the skin, break the flesh, dig in. The splinter is stubborn. It happened as I maneuvered the floorboard back into place. Fourth finger. Right hand.

I have rinsed my hair and dried it. It is not as "ash" as the wig. It will do; it is different enough. It is the difference that counts.

I put the wig with the dress on the bed.

The phone rings.

"Hello."

"Is Steven there, please?" A male voice, well spoken, polite.

"I think you have the wrong number."

"Sorry to disturb you."

When I dial 1471 to get the caller's number, the mechanical female voice says, "The caller withheld their number."

The phone rings again.

"Hello."

"Is Steven there, please?" The same male voice.

"I'm afraid he's not in at the moment. Can I take a message?" I put on a fake foreign accent. A mixture of German and French.

"Can you tell him Dumont rang?" Wherever he is, someone opens a door, a hum of chatter bursts through. The door closes again.

"Your number?"

"He has my number, tell him it's urgent."

"Have you tried his mobile?"

"I can't get through."

"I'll pass the message."

"Thank you."

"Good-bye."

"Good-bye."

I get the number of the hotel from Directory Inquiries. Before I dial it, I dial 141 to withhold my number.

The female says, "The Charles Hotel, can I help you?"

"Could I speak with Dumont, please?"

"Who's calling?"

"Sophia Lawrence."

I am put on hold. Classical music plays.

"Hello." The same male voice as before.

I put the phone down.

Ylang-ylang for shock.

Tangerine for emotional emptiness.

Rosemary for disorientation.

The oils are effective: I am neither languid with despair nor rigid with anger.

"Steven": the name he must use for "other" work. It does not have the same panache.

The curtain billows in, skims the side of my bare arm.

I close my eyes and listen to the chimes. Let the sound of them fill me. They seem to get louder the longer I listen. They move between three notes. Two high and a low. They seem to move farther away.

I was waking when I saw her. I was not sure if I was dreaming. The treatment door was open. Sophia walking past the doorway. Blond and purple. A dream, I thought. I am dreaming. I closed my eyes. Wondered how long I had been asleep. Heard the roll and click of a lighter. Smelled cigarette smoke.

"Skye?" I called out.

I can hear her moving up the passageway toward me.

She stands in the doorway, weight on one leg, hips and breasts pronounced and made shiny by the purple silk.

There is no doubt she makes a better Sophia than I do.

She strikes another pose. Arm stretched up along the doorframe. Face turned to profile.

I notice there is a series of small bruises on her right upper arm. She turns to look at me.

"I guessed it was you that rang me last night," she says. "You want to know why he rang me?" she adds. "He asked me not to tell you. He thought it would upset you. The dress," she says. "Ivan wanted me to come and help him buy the dress. I told him purple was not a color either of us wore," she says.

I watch her as she changes back into her own clothes. I had got up and told her to please take the wig and the dress off, led her into the bedroom. In my mouth I can taste blood from where I have bitten the inside of my cheek too hard.

Skye picks up the dress from the floor and passes it to me, watching me as I carefully place it back on the bed and smooth it out.

"Did it do the trick?" she asks.

"Yes, thank you. It did the trick."

"I need a cigarette," she says, and she leaves the room.

I pick up the wig, brush it out, put it into the box that it came in.

We sit in the kitchen, drinking coffee, not talking. The phone suddenly rings. Telephones always suddenly ring. There is never a warning. Or it is the warning.

Skye sees I make no effort to get it, leans back in her chair and picks up the receiver.

"Hello," she says.

"You must have the wrong number," she says, and she puts the phone down.

"Did they ask for Steven?" I ask her.

She nods her head.

The phone rings again. This time Skye leaves it. We watch as the answerphone clicks to messages.

"Steven, this is Dumont. I've had some very interesting news. It would be nice if we could discuss it." His tone is sarcastic.

"'Dumont' is the gambler," I tell Skye as the tape rewinds. "Ivan is Steven. The money is counterfeit."

Skye opens her mouth, looks as if she is about to say something. Changes her mind.

She looks at her watch. "I have to go now, Stella," she says.

I see her to the front door.

As she walks down the stairs, she stops and turns. "Stella," she says, "Dumont is not a gambler. Dumont is a very dangerous man. Ivan doesn't know what he's got himself into."

I ask her, "What do you mean?"

But she turns and keeps walking down the stairs.

I watch her from the balcony as she gets into her car and drives away.

I have tried to ring her on her mobile but it is only taking messages.

I ring Ivan, but I can't get through.

I ring the hotel. Dumont will not be available this afternoon, I am told. I am asked, "Would you like to leave a message?"

"No. No thank you," and I put the phone down.

I go out onto the balcony. Skye has left her cigarettes.

The sound of classical music. Something with a lot of strings. It is coming from the open sunroof of a large silver-blue car with tinted windows. The car is cruising slowly up the street, carefully negotiating the speed bumps. A couple of houses on, the car stops. Then reverses. It comes to a halt opposite the main front door; after a moment it pulls over to park on the other side of the road. The engine is turned off. The car fan whining as it cools down. The music continues to play.

The car doors open; shoes glint in the late-afternoon light. The driver is a young man with a shaved head. The passenger is an older man, fifties, perhaps. Their suits—expensive.

I watch them, wait for them to cross the road, come up the path and ring the bell; they will no doubt ask for Steven, tell me Dumont has sent them. Information will be exchanged.

They aren't crossing the road; they are taking off their jackets and opening the back doors of the car and getting out hangers and hanging their jackets up, leaning in to place them on hooks that must be there just above the windows. They are obviously intending to wait for Ivan outside; they are anticipating a long wait.

They have got back into the car, opened the windows.

I watch them. They roll up the cuffs of their shirts and check their watches. I check my watch. Five o'clock. The music has been turned off to take a phone call. The conversation consists of a series of "Yep"s and "Yeah"s, laughter and then "Laters," like Skye says it. It should be "Later." No *s*. The driver looks up at me for a moment, then looks away as he puts the phone down.

. . .

They've been sitting there for ten minutes now.

In the car the men have turned the radio on. Faint strains of a phone-in show. They laugh simultaneously at something. The older man bangs his fist against the open window frame. The younger man creases forward and rests his head on the steering wheel. It is half past five.

Catrina Heksa has come out onto her balcony; she nods to me across the railings; she has noticed the car.

"Do you think they're the police?" she says.

I shrug my shoulders.

Below, a car door slams closed; we both look across. The older man has got out and is walking as if to cross the road. But he stops at the front of the car, leans against the bonnet, lights a cigarette, holding his hand around the flame even though the air is still enough to cut. He tilts his head up as he takes a drag, makes no effort to look away

I look away, casually deadhead a nasturtium.

"They must be waiting for someone to come home," says Catrina Heksa.

I suspect she has been eavesdropping.

"Is George with you?" I ask her as a way of changing the subject.

"Who?"

"My cat."

"Oh, you mean 'Kitty,'" she says.

She turns, disappears into her flat, reappears with George cradled in her arms.

"Sorry—he came in this morning. He's been sleeping on my bed."

She puts George down; he gives me a lazy sideways glance, stretches, yawns and turns, walks back into Catrina Heksa's flat.

"Do you want me to bring him over?"

"He'll come for his food," I tell her.

"Tell me if you change your mind," she says as she moves inside.

Below in the street the man flicks away his finished cigarette. He seems to take pride in the act, watches it as it arcs the entire width of the road. Lands in the gutter. He looks up, winks and gets back into the car.

George saunters over at six prompt. I follow him into the kitchen, open him a tin of sardines. Add a sprinkle of catnip. Rub his ears while he eats. He finishes eating, saunters out and turns right. I try Skye's phone again. It goes to messages.

I go out onto the balcony again to see the younger man emerging from behind the privet hedge of one of the larger houses, zipping up his fly. The older man is out of the car too, smoking another cigarette. He flicks it away. They both get back into the car. They have changed the radio channel back to classical.

It is half past six. George is sleeping on Catrina Heksa's balcony. I make the kissing noise. His right ear twitches, but that is all. The older man gets out of the car and lights a cigarette. I turn to look at the telephone and think about what I would say to Ivan:

"There has been a car parked here all afternoon with two men sitting in it."

And he would remain silent.

"Ivan—they're waiting for you."

I run to the phone, dial his number.

He says, "Sweetheart." And then it goes dead.

The older man has got back into the car when I return.

Ivan's van is pulling into the street. The men in the car open their respective doors and get out. The younger man puts his hands in his pockets; the middle-aged man lights another cigarette. They cross the road as Ivan parks.

Ivan steps out onto the pavement. He doesn't seem surprised to see them, leans to one side to put his toolbox down as they approach. I think I see him smile. But he looks anxious. He offers his hand as if in greeting, but the older man is making jabbing motions toward him with his cigarette.

"You've let us down, Steven. We are disappointed in you, Steven. We expected more from you," he says.

The younger man has stopped a pace behind the older man; he says nothing.

Ivan is offering explanations; I can tell by the way he is moving his hands. Circling them around each other, one direction and then the other.

The older man shouts, "Steven! You fucked up!"

Ivan folds his arms. He looks nervous. He glances up and

sees me, lifts an index finger and moves it side to side. The slightest of gestures. One I know: Keep quiet. Shut up. He is about to talk again, unfolds his arms. The older man flicks his cigarette away, takes a step back; the younger man steps forward, stands square in front of Ivan. There is a moment of silence as they stare at each other, and then he punches Ivan in the stomach. Ivan curls forward, falls on his knees and then to the left. The man squats down beside Ivan, rolls him and pulls at him to open his jacket. Searching the pockets, he finds and removes a brown envelope. He stands and kicks Ivan twice, so hard it makes his body shift across the pavement. Ivan brings his knees up to his chest, curls up into a ball. The older man is saying, "You should've been more careful, Steven. You've only got yourself to blame. You fucked up." The younger man is looking at the contents of the envelope; he nods his head at the older man. They turn, casually walk back to their car and put on their jackets. A swift three-point turn and they are gone.

Catrina Heksa's voice: "Should I call the police?"

"No." I do not look at her.

I look at Ivan; he does not move.

Underneath my concern there are other thoughts. Thoughts I shouldn't be thinking; what I witnessed is punishment for Ivan. For taking Skye with him to buy the dress. For lying to me about Canada. And the money.

I felt, within all the horror of it, pleasure. Enjoyment even.

My feelings are twisting to guilt: below on the street, Ivan's body is twitching like he is dreaming. I turn and walk into the kitchen and then into the passageway; I increase my pace, grab the rucksack. Open the door. I take the stairs two at a time. The squeak of my hand against the banister filling the stairwell. Before I know it, I'm on the path outside. Running very fast. And then stopping. Standing very still.

In the middle of the road, Skye's car, driver's door open, engine still running.

On the pavement, Ivan.

Skye kneeling in front of Ivan.

She is trying to help him to stand. He is resisting. Pushing her away, extricating himself from her grasp, from her two hands wrapped around his right upper arm. He slumps the side of his body against his van, hands on his stomach, head down, slides his body upright.

I can see his face. I cannot see her face. They do not seem to see me. They do not seem to hear me as I walk down the path. He is saying, quietly, but I can hear it, I can make out the words, "Why don't you just fuck off?" She stands, says his name softly, the *I* of "Ivan" lost in her throat, touches his shoulder. He shrugs her off, lifts his head; his eyes are wide with adrenaline. He is regarding her with contempt. She is turning her head away from Ivan, biting her bottom lip. She is crying. She has seen me, standing where I've stopped at the end of the path. We stand as if frozen. Ivan smiles when he sees me. I wait for the panic attack, but it doesn't come.

I don't know how long we stand like this.

Skye is touching him again. Her hand on his shoulder. He removes her hand. Approaches me with his hands outstretched as if he is going to lead me to dance. Skye won't look at me; she walks in the other direction to her car, gets in, drives away.

"Sweetheart," he says.

"Are you all right?"

"I will be."

His embrace is too tight.

He held me tight for a long time.

He pulled away, held me by the arms. He looked at the bracelet on my wrist.

"I didn't expect the questions. Our arrangement."

He released a hand, motioned it between his chest and mine. He stroked my hair.

"I didn't expect you. . . ." He smiled. "You look nice," he said.

He stroked my hair again, turned and walked down the ramp to the garage underneath the flats.

I watched him as he disappeared into the darkness.

I stood and I waited. I heard an electronic beep. Heard locks sliding. Saw lights go on and then off. The hum of an engine.

A black car with tinted windows slowly emerged.

He drew up beside me. His window was rolled down. He was wearing a jacket I had never seen before. Black. Leather. Soft. Italian. Inside the car the glove compartment was open. A barrel of a gun peeped out.

"You have a gun?" I said.

The creases at the sides of his eyes narrowed, folded into

each other, as he began to smile. The car still slowly moving, creeping away.

"Bond always has a gun, Miss Moneypenny." Scottish accent thick. "I'll call you," he said.

I watched him drive to the bottom of the street. The indicator blinked five times. He turned left and was gone.

I turned, looked up at my balcony with its yellow and orange and red nasturtiums.

Catrina Heksa was on her balcony. In her arms was George. She said nothing.

I walked up the path. Let myself in. The door closed quietly behind me. I walked up the stairs. Opened my flat door. Went inside. Closed the door. Double-locked it.

Ivan didn't ask me to go with him. The disappointment is larger than the relief. On the passenger seat in the car I saw the cigar box.

He is not coming back.

I wait for the smell of gas to come. Wait for it, faint then stronger as it always comes. I wait but it doesn't come.

I walk into each room in turn. Sniff the air.

Just the smell of geranium I was burning earlier.

I do not feel thankful; it is a sign. It makes me nervous.

I fold laundry very carefully. Run my hand across each crease. Smooth out with both hands. Set accurate piles of T-shirts, socks, pants. Arrange them neatly in the drawers of the bedside chest.

. . .

I go into each room again, rearrange an item. Set it straight or crooked. I wipe down all the surfaces in the kitchen. And the bathroom.

I sit in the kitchen. Drink chamomile tea. The emptiness of the flat closes in on me, presses against my chest and my back; my arms, my legs, the sides of my face. It moves away, expanding. It moves down the passageway, settles under chairs and the tables, in the gaps between the bottles of oil in the cabinet, the cups in the kitchen cupboard, the space underneath the bed, the space under the floorboards. It finds walls and doors and windows, gets restless, comes back to me and presses itself against my limbs. Moves away again. Comes back. It is slow and continuous. I walk down the passageway. Close all the doors to all the rooms. Go back to the kitchen. Sit down.

Downstairs someone is having a shower. Two floors down, someone is watering their plants and talking to someone inside the flat. Somewhere else a television is on. Someone else is playing music and singing along to the words. Motown. Supremes. "Stop! In the Name of Love." I know the words. A verse occupies my time. I can hear Catrina Heksa come out onto her balcony. She calls, "Sophia." And then she calls, "Stella." I don't answer. She knocks something as she moves back inside; it falls and breaks and she swears. I am aware of the emptiness in the flat tightening; it will get worse once it gets dark. I turn lights on in preparation.

There is only bread and cheese to eat. Or the oranges. I make a sandwich, take one bite, throw it away.

I go out onto the balcony, kiss for George but he does not come.

I burn marjoram; this is supposed to be the remedy for loneliness. I didn't think it would come this quick.

Berlin . . . Budapest . . . Prague . . . Amsterdam . . . Africa . . . Canada? I turn the pages of the atlas.

I think It would not be much different being on the run. Moving swiftly, keeping all contact, eyes and otherwise, furtive and to the minimum. It would not be much different. From being here. From staying still.

The bath salts are white, but they turn the water turquoise blue. Turquoise is known to help feelings of loneliness and to give confidence to those who are trying to make a new start. This is what it says on the jar's label. Turquoise like the sea around the island in the Indian Ocean. The one I saw on television. I sense a restlessness move through my body, but I stay in the bath until it grows cold. I still can't smell gas.

It is ten o'clock. There has been no phone call. No message.

The computer says it takes less than half an hour to walk the perimeter of the island. In the same amount of time I have rung all my clients and told them I will no longer be practicing. Some of them seemed upset.

For the last hour I have cried.

I unpack my rucksack. Repack. Replace some items. I have done it twice. I stare at the telephone. Will it to ring.

The flats are quiet now. Everyone is sleeping. I have taken five drops of Rescue Remedy. Twenty of valerian.

I turn off all the lights, thinking perhaps it may be easier not to see anything.

I go outside and sit on the balcony. It has been raining; the air is damp. I watch as other lights go out in the city skyline. Two cars glide quietly into the wet street. Park opposite the path. Men get out. Move silently up the path in single file. In one of the cars, someone remains, opens the window. The faint but familiar clink of bangles. An orange glow as a cigarette is lit.

Someone has let the men in the main front door. Or someone has given them the key. I can hear the stairs creak gently under their weight as I walk down the passageway. I stand there. Wait.

They ring the bell. They knock. They try a credit card to open the locks; it does not work.

The wood on the doorframe splits as they jimmy it open.

They showed IDs and the search warrant.

"Stella Lewis?" one of them said.

"Sister of Skye Lewis? Partner of Ivan Turner?" another added.

They talked in a manner they thought they ought to. I could do this too.

"That is correct."

I sat with two of them at the kitchen table; they weren't wearing uniforms. They sat opposite me and stared at me.

The others were searching the flat; I could hear cupboards and drawers being opened. I could hear floorboards being lifted and turned. I could hear things being put into clear polythene bags. I heard "We've found his van" come through on a number of walkie-talkies.

"I don't know where he is," I said.

"We haven't asked you where he is," one of them said.

I knew then they already had him.

I made them tea.

One of the men had a large manila envelope; he removed something from it, put it onto the table, pushed it to the middle.

"Do you recognize this woman?"

A photograph. Skye as Sophia, purple, blond, lips dark and prominent, sitting on a green sofa, a chandelier in the background.

"It is my sister," I told them.

He laid out more pictures, taken at short intervals; like a small movie.

Skye stands; she is smiling.

Ivan walks into frame.

Skye and Ivan embrace.

Skye and Ivan kiss. A passionate kiss.

Skye and Ivan sitting down.

Ivan's hand being placed tenderly on her cheek.

Ivan's hand moving hair from her face.

Skye leaning her head into his hand. Kissing his hand.

Ivan is wearing the leather jacket. From his pocket he takes an envelope.

He hands the envelope to Skye.

She bends forward, opens her bag, places the envelope inside.

More people entering the frame.

The two men that beat Ivan up.

Dumont.

They greet Skye with kisses to each cheek. They shake Ivan's hand.

"We've known about their operation for some time," the detective said. He gathered up the pictures. I thought that was it, but he was only making room for more.

"This was taken yesterday," he said as he laid down the first.

Ivan and Skye; Skye as Skye, in an alley arguing. Skye looks furious. In one of Ivan's hands, a bag, the one the dress came in, his other hand tight around her arm, holding her at arm's length as he tries to stop her taking the bag, her skin denting under his grip.

The detective dealt out five more pictures like he was playing cards.

"These were taken today."

. . .

Skye on the balcony, before she had changed.

Me on the balcony.

The two men in the car.

Ivan being beaten up.

Ivan driving away.

"Skye told Dumont Ivan had come to see us. She told Dumont Ivan had betrayed them. We didn't know she was going to do that."

They saw me look at the photograph of Skye and Ivan arguing.

"It's a little complicated," one of them said.

"She got a little . . . jealous, should we say," the other added.
He picked up the photograph of Ivan being hit. He looked at
my hair.

"Didn't you used to be a redhead?"

The two detectives smiled at each other. One of them
winked.

They stared at me again.

A minute passed.

"She wanted us to let you know, wanted to put you in the
picture, so to speak. . . ." He laughed at his own pun.

Someone shouted in from the passageway, "Nothing,
guv," like they do on television.

The detectives gathered up the photographs, shoved them
back into the manila envelope, stood up, pushed back their
chairs.

"She came to us because of you," the one who winked said. "We should thank you."

"You speeded up the operation," the other one said, hand on my arm.

I followed them down the passageway and stepped out onto the landing, watched them take the stairs.

One of them looked back. "A man has been called to fix the door," he said.

I ran down the passageway to watch them from the balcony. A hint of something floral as a car door was opened and the light came on.

The door closing, a cigarette being thrown from the window.

The cars left the street as quietly as they came.

I moved slowly through the flat. Went from room to room.

I straightened furniture and closed drawers and cupboard doors. They had taken the computer and the client files.

I did the trick of asking myself what I was going to think of next to stop myself thinking.

They had left the rucksack; the contents spilled on the bedroom floor.

I put a book against the front door to try to close it.

I repacked my rucksack slowly and carefully.

I got ready the tea tree cream and a plaster.

Using the sharpest knife, I cut the last undamaged finger.

On the computer they will find the copy I made of Ivan's disk. No doubt they will be able to open it.

. . .

The man has come to fix new locks on my door. I stand in the passageway and watch him as he works. He is tall. A little younger than me. His eyes are brown. He works quickly with his electric drill and electric screwdriver. There is no wedding ring on his ring finger. No evidence of a woman in his life: a dull grayness to his "white" T-shirt. He has smiled at me each time he has looked at me. I have smiled back.

"Would you like a cup of tea?"

He says, "Yes, please."

"Do you take sugar?"

He takes two and a half sugars.

I make two cups of tea. Add two sugars to one of them and stir it. It is the first thing I have to do. Wean him off the sugar.

"You lived here long?"

"Yes."

We both take a sip of tea. He looks past me into the bedroom.

"Nice place—do you live alone?"

The man who has fixed my door searches my eyes with his as he waits for me to answer. The phone has begun to ring. It goes to answerphone. Skye's voice comes from the kitchen. Vowels soft and throaty.

"Stella. Pick up the phone. We need to talk. Pick up the phone, Stella. Pick up the phone."

She stops talking. Waits. Hangs up.

He waits for my answer. He drains his cup of tea. Puts the cup on the floor.

I am standing very close to him. Close enough to feel the heat off his body. He still waits for my answer.

If I say yes, if he comes to live with me . . .

. . . there will still be Skye. All sweet. Up to her old tricks.

I shake my head.

I close the front door behind him. Listen to him as he takes the stairs, wait for the sound of the main front door as it closes.

The new sets of keys grow warm in my hand. I open the fist I have made around them. Look at the imprint they have already made on my palm. I look at the door they are waiting to lock.

I turn and look down the passageway. All the doors to the rooms are open. The emptiness comes again from each room, presses itself against my chest.

I move down the passageway into the kitchen, go on to the balcony, kiss for George.

He doesn't come.

Down in the street, Ivan's van is still there.

I close the balcony doors.

Shut the cat flap.

I gather together documents and put them into envelopes.

It feels strange to double-lock the front door from outside. Across the landing I hear the floorboards creak behind Catrina Heksa's door.

Catrina Heksa has opened her door before I have even knocked. She opens the door wider to allow for the ruck-sack. George is in the passageway; he patters forward to

meet me and head-butts each of my feet; I kneel down, rub
his ears.

Behind me Catrina Heksa closes the door. I can feel her
staring at my back. "I didn't tell the police about the letter,"
she says.

I turn and smile my thanks. "It wouldn't have made any
difference."

She looks at the floor. "I thought you might have thought
it was me who called the police."

I say nothing.

"Would you like a coffee?" she says after a moment.

We sit on the edge of her bed and drink the coffee. George
lies between us; we take our turns stroking him. He purrs
loudly, indifferent to this silent exchange of cat ownership.
He catches my eye, looks at me like the first time we met. I
enter the realm of the eternal; he arches his back, takes his
look to her, her eyes already waiting. The exchange is complete. I feel suddenly tired.

"Can I lie down for a while?" I ask her.

She leans back, plumps up a pillow for me, leaves the
room; George trots after her. I close my eyes. As I fall asleep,
I hear her talking to someone on the telephone, telling someone she misses him or her. If I go outside I will be unable to
miss Ivan; I have never known him out there.

Her back is to me when I wake. Stretching with slow
breaths, George sleeps by her chest. The balcony doors are
open. It is not quite light yet. The air grainy and gray and

still. I get up quietly, creep down the passageway, collect my rucksack and go to the bathroom.

I comb my hair and put in my green eyes. I cover the bruise with makeup. Carefully outline my lips with the Raspberry lipstick. I look at my feet. My sensible loafers. I don't want to wear them. Not anymore.

In the passageway Catrina Heksa's sandals are lined up in front of the mirror. In white and in silver and in black. She will not mind, I think. She will understand. I slip off my shoes. I was going to put on the white version. I put on the silver version. Pull the straps over my heels.

On the table in the kitchen I leave the two envelopes. One contains George's insurance documents, the details of his vet. The other, instructions to let, spare keys, details of where to bank the money, a check for her trouble. I take the dried cat food out of the rucksack and leave it on the floor.

I slip the straps of the rucksack over my shoulders; turn back for a moment to where they are sleeping. George is in the bedroom doorway. He scratches his ear, begins to clean himself. I open the door while he isn't looking, pull it to as quietly as I can.

I look across the landing to the door of my flat. I think I can hear the emptiness in the flat humming. A soft, hardly discernible hum coming from behind the closed door. What remains of me there, suffused in the walls and the furniture, is evaporating and fading. I turn away. I look at my feet in the silver sling-back sandals.

I count the steps. Twenty to the second floor. Twenty to
the first. Twenty. Ground. The black and white tiles. I open

the door; it is heavier than I remember. The sound of my heels goes *click click click* as I walk down the path and up the street. The lamps on the street switch off as I walk. The sun is rising.

I touch the first lamppost as I pass it, keep my focus on the second, feel the firmness of the stone beneath my feet. At the second lamppost, I notice I am limping but I am not worried; it is only slight. The breeze is fresh. Pulls the hair from my face and neck. I think it will rain soon: I can hear trains in the distance. I untuck my hair from behind my ear. The bracelet shifts on my arm; I smile: I have a new name. As I reach the third lamppost, I am no longer limping; the panic is leaving. I walk to the end of the street. I turn left. In the sky a plane's lights. Red and white. Blinking.

ACKNOWLEDGMENTS

For their helpfulness and support, I am grateful to the following: Jenny Ashworth, Rosie and Jessica Buckman, Christina Dunhill, Victoria Millar, Laura Morris, Alexandra Pringle, Chiki Sarkar and Miles Visman. Also, I would like to thank London Arts for their financial assistance.

Not forgetting special mention to sources consulted: *Aromatherapy for the Family,* Jan Kusmirek, ed. (Wigmore Publications Limited, 1997); *The SAS Survival Handbook,* John "Lofty" Wiseman (HarperCollins, 1999).

For U.S. publication, my thanks and appreciation to: Molly Barton, Carole DeSanti, and Irene Skolnick.